SERVANT, MERCENARY, BROTHER

Vol. I

The Mercenary and the Mage series
suggested reading order:

Servant, Mercenary, Brother:
A Dresden Jakobs Vignette Collection Volume I

Prince of Shadow and Ash
(The Mercenary and the Mage Book 1)

Staff of Nightfall
(The Mercenary and the Mage Book 2)

Servant, Mercenary, Brother:
A Dresden Jakobs Vignette Collection Volume II

Bells of Winter: A Mercenary and the Mage Story

Also from Selina R. Gonzalez:
The Miraveld Chronicles
A Thieving Curse

The Dragon Prince's Heart:
An A Thieving Curse *Companion Novella*

A Lonely Dance

Be sure to follow Selina on social media to stay
up-to-date on all book-related news!

SelinaRGonzalez.com
Facebook.com/SelinaRGonzalez
Instagram.com/NightTooIsBeautiful

SERVANT, MERCENARY, BROTHER

A Dresden Jakobs
Vignette Collection
Volume I

Selina R. Gonzalez

First paperback edition February 2020
First published in ebook October 2019

ISBN 978-1-7344676-0-4

Published by Wyvern Wing Press
www.WyvernWingPress.com
www.SelinaRGonzalez.com

To those who love me when I feel unlovable and believe in me when I don't believe in myself, especially my sisters by blood and in spirit: Rebecca, Jessica, Sylvia, and Alexis.

CONTENTS

Map ii

Contract... 1

Eyes Down 11

Drown 17

Trouble 23

The River.. 35

Let's Be Mercenaries 45

Caught Shirking 51

Changes 61

Crime & Punishment 67

Horse Thief... 77

Picking Up Strays 87

The Letter... 99

My Lord.. 107

MAP

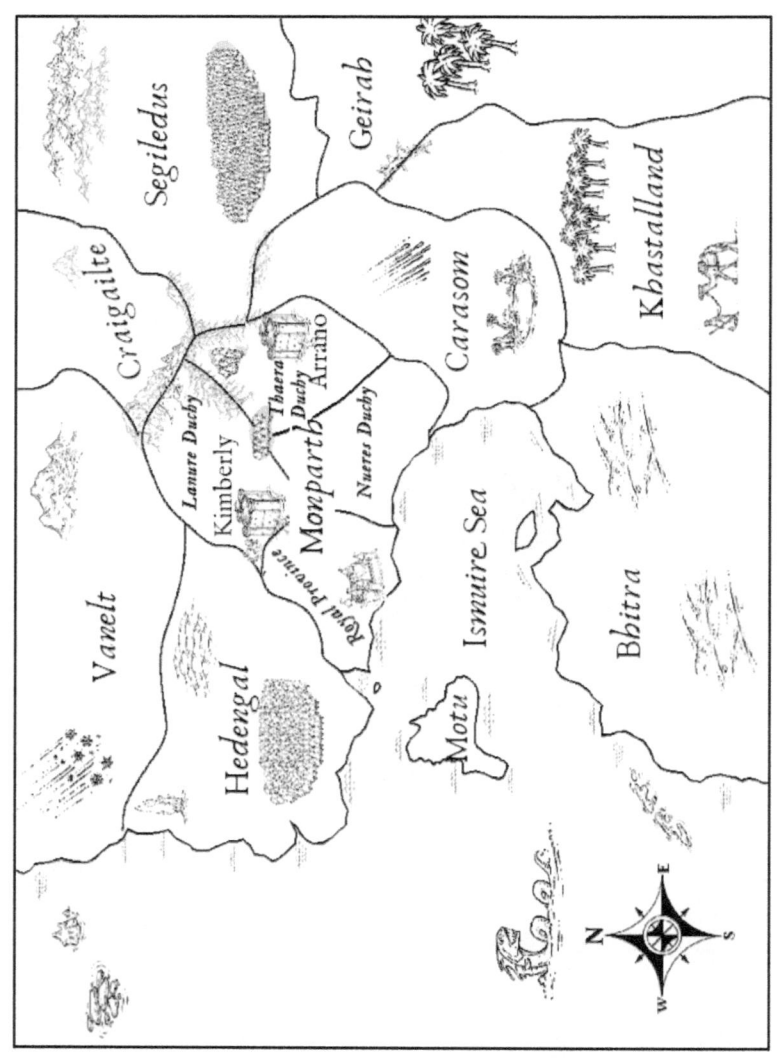

Contract

Dresden, Age: 10
Location: Lanure Duchy, Monparth

A loud thud sounded from the tiny kitchen and Dresden paused outside the back door. His grip tightened on the basket of eggs as Da's agitated voice filtered through the uneven gaps in the rough wood door of their mud cottage.

"I don't know what else to do!" Da snapped in Carasian. Whatever they were arguing about, it was bad if Da wasn't using Monparthian. Da had a rule: between breakfast and supper, only Monparthian. He wanted his family to do well in Monparth.

Wanted. Dresden didn't understand the specifics, but he knew they weren't doing well. Ma and Da argued more all the time. It scared little four-year-old Tatya, and Dresden hated that. But he didn't know what the problem was, other than they were in trouble, so he didn't know how to fix it. He knew that they didn't have the coin to replace the trousers that showed his ankles, that Ma had added fabric from an apron to the sleeves and sides of Tatya's dress when it got too tight instead of replacing it.

"But the animals are the only thing keeping us going," Ma said quietly, also in Carasian. "What will we do without selling the milk and eggs? How will we feed the children? We will have nothing."

A shudder went through Dresden. He brushed dark hair out of his eyes as he glanced back at the little pen, where Tatya was cooing under her breath to the goat while stroking its black hair. The nanny goat mostly ignored her, contentedly chewing on grass. Da wanted to sell the animals? *But...what will we eat? And Tatya is going to cry.*

"We'll still have a home," Da said roughly. "They keep increasing the interest, saying there's a new fee. They're robbing us, and I can't...no official will listen to a Carasian peasant. If I don't sell the animals now, they'll take them and throw us out." Da drew a ragged breath. "I'm sorry. I failed you. We shouldn't have left Carasom. I shouldn't have taken us so far into Monparth—"

"My beloved, hush." Soft footsteps sounded on the dirt floor of the kitchen, and Dresden leaned closer to the door. "Our children have been spared the violence we suffered."

"We could have gone somewhere else," Da mumbled. "Other parts of Carasom have better rulers, who keep better peace. Or we could have—"

"We are here now. We cannot move forward by dwelling on the past, because we cannot change it. You did what you thought was right. I trusted you. I still trust you."

Dresden nudged the door, and it inched open. He peered through the narrow gap. Ma stood next to Da, who sat at the rough square table, his head in his hands. She tenderly stroked his thick dark hair, but her olive brown face was drawn and oddly pale.

"You believe this is best?" Ma murmured. "It will be enough silver?"

Da's shoulders heaved. "If we sell them all? The cow, the chickens, the goat... I think so. We'll find a way to survive. It will be easier without them taking every spare coin."

Ma's lower lip trembled, but she nodded. "Then that's what we'll do."

When they didn't say anything more, Dresden finally pushed open the door and walked in, pretending like he hadn't just heard that Da was selling all their animals, that they weren't about to lose almost everything. He smiled as well as he could.

"I got all the eggs," he said in Monparthian. "Twenty today. How many should I put aside for the market?"

Da lifted his head. "None of them, Dresden." His Monparthian was thick and heavily accented. His dark eyes looked tired. "Leave them on the table for your mother. I need you to help me take the cow and goat into town. We'll be taking the chickens in tomorrow."

Dresden froze. He wanted to ask why, to know what was happening. But demanding answers of his father would not be respectful. "Yes, Da."

Tatya did cry when Dresden took the goat from her pen and Ma explained the goat had to leave and not come back. She clung to Ma's skirts, snot running from her little button nose. It twisted Dresden's heart.

They led the red heifer and the black nanny goat into town and walked the three miles along the worn, rutted road in silence. Da's scimitars across his back glinted in the midday sun. Dresden wished he could wear his.

3

Da looked so intimidating wearing them. But despite Da giving him his own set last year, Dresden wasn't very good with them yet. They were still big for him to use and made him tired.

The tangle of wooden buildings forming the town of Wiltsley spread out ahead of them. The air took on a stench of bodies and waste that Dresden hated as they drew closer. Da sighed.

"Dresden... I want you to understand. So you never do what I did." Da rubbed the back of his neck with his free hand, the other holding the lead to the heifer. "I borrowed coin to get us started here. Too much. And I took too long to pay it back. We desperately need coin—" Da drew in a sharp breath and stopped short. "Dresden. Stay close to me."

Dresden took in his father's tense expression, then traced his stare to two Monparthian men walking toward them. One was broad-shouldered, dressed in rich linens dyed deep blues and greens, his blond hair drawn back in a greasy tail. The other was slim, with an overly wide smile, wiry brown eyebrows, and closely-shorn brown hair.

"Jakobs, fancy seeing you here," Blond said, a mocking edge to his voice. "This must be your son?" He looked to Dresden. Dresden drew closer to Da's side.

"Where are you going with those fine animals?" Skinny asked.

"Market," Da said flatly.

"I see." Blond stopped, entirely too close for Dresden's comfort. "Hopefully they fetch a good price, if you're to pay back the two hundred and fifty silver you owe."

"Two—it's one hundred and eighty," Da exclaimed.

Skinny shrugged. "Pretty sure with your current interest and fees for our time, I have two hundred and fifty written down. You might be in luck, though." Skinny stepped closer. "How old are you, boy?" The man reached toward Dresden, and Da stepped between them.

"Don't touch my son."

Dresden peered around Da's shoulder, squeezing the goat's lead so hard the rope dug into his palms.

Skinny held up his hands. "Easy, I'm not threatening. Just thinking." He nodded toward town. "There's a man in town from the Kimberly estate. They're looking for a boy between the ages of nine and twelve to be a personal manservant to some noble boy."

Dresden wrinkled his nose. *A servant to some stuck-up noble?*

"Hey, that's smart, Jeffrey," Blond said. "Come on. We'll take you to him."

"I'm not interested," Da said. He started forward, and the men blocked his path.

"Wearing your weapons again, I see," Skinny—Jeffrey, apparently—said.

Da shifted. He wasn't nervous...was he? Da was never nervous. Dresden peered up at Da's strained expression.

"Surprised you haven't sold those yet," Jeffrey continued. "Hardly proper for a peasant to be caring them around. Someone might think you're trying to cause trouble. Mightn't they, Trenton?"

"Aye, they might."

"No trouble." Da's throat bobbed.

"Good," Trenton said. "Then you'll happily accompany us." The men started forward. Da hesitated, then fol-

5

lowed. Dresden trailed after him, the goat nudging his hip with her head.

These were the men Da owed? *Why would Da ever make a deal with people like that?*

The men led them past the marketplace to a tavern. A few people stood around under the wood awning stretching across the front of the tall, narrow building. Blond waved at a middle-aged man with a pinched expression who was shaking his head at a couple of young men. He shooed the young men away and crossed over.

"Can I help you?"

"You're the man from the Kimberly estate, yes?" Trenton asked.

The man lifted a brow. "I'm Steward Harreldon, yes."

"Heard you were looking for a servant boy." Trenton jerked his thumb toward Dresden. "Might have found one. Depends on the deal."

"No," Da said, his voice steady. "This is a misunderstanding."

"Might change your mind depending on the deal," Jeffrey said.

Harreldon ran a palm over his flashy bright green doublet, looking down his nose at all of them. "Lord Kimberly has in his care a young...nobleman. He's eleven and requires a servant of a similar age. Someone to do his cleaning and wait on him, accompany him, do whatever small tasks the young man might require. The terms are a ten-year indenture, purchased for four hundred silver, paid to the boy's family."

Dresden's eyes went wide. *Four hundred silver!*

"Well, that seems excellent." Jeffrey turned toward Da. "You can send your boy to serve some rich nobleman's son, keep your animals, get a little extra coin, and we get our three hundred silver."

"Three hundred?" Da's voice squeaked.

Trenton grinned, the look somehow savage. "Middleman fee for arranging this deal."

"And if I say no?" Da said quietly.

"Well, we still went to all this trouble," Jeffrey said with the fakest expression of concern Dresden had ever seen, "so you'll still owe us three hundred."

Dresden coiled and uncoiled the rope in his hands. Would...would Da send him away? For ten years? *Tatya could get a new dress. Ma and Da could stop fighting. Da wouldn't have to sell the animals.*

"What is indenture?" Dresden asked. His voice sounded small and high, and he tried to cover it by standing up straighter.

Harreldon clasped his hands behind his back. "A contract that binds you to your master until you've repaid the debt, fulfilled the terms of your contract, and your master signs your release. In this case, ten years in exchange for four hundred silver. If you leave before you are released, you will be hunted, and your master can choose to take you back or have you imprisoned or executed."

Dresden swallowed hard.

"Thank you for your time." Da inclined his head, but Dresden caught the slight tremor in his voice. "We are not interested."

Jeffrey looked askance at Trenton. "Shame. Hope you can get three hundred silver for your animals. Better sell the foreign swords, too. Maybe that will get you close." He lifted a shoulder.

Da just nodded and turned back toward the market. Dresden followed slowly. "Da?"

"Yes?"

"Can you get three hundred silver for the animals?"

Da's shoulders slumped. "No."

Dresden's feet dragged, his worn boots catching on the uneven street. *Da wanted to sell the animals so he wouldn't owe coin. And he still will.* "Da?"

"Yes, Dresden."

"Will they really make us leave the house?"

Da stopped short and gave Dresden a sharp look. "Were you listening to your ma and I talk?"

Dresden's cheeks heated, and he ducked his head.

"Possibly," Da said with a sigh.

And Tatya won't have a safe home. Dresden straightened and lifted his chin. "I can be a servant."

Da's eyes widened. "Dresden, no—"

But Dresden dropped the goat's lead and ran back to the man in the fancy doublet. Harreldon lifted a brow as Dresden stopped in front of him. "I will do it."

"No." Da's hand clamped his shoulder and pulled him back.

Dresden turned on him. "Tatya should be able to get a new dress. And Ma is right. You need the animals. Please, Da."

Da's eyes glistened. "You don't understand what you're saying."

Maybe he didn't. He wasn't sure. He'd heard nobles could be rude. Mean. But those men were mean to Da. And Dresden could make them leave Da alone. "I will do it."

Harreldon grunted. "Your father has to agree. You both have to sign the papers."

"And the silver coin?" Dresden asked.

"Locked up in the tavern."

Da shuffled his feet. "So if we agreed...you would give me the coin today?" He shook his head. "No. I can't. Dresden, your ma will never forgive me."

"What will happen to Ma if you can't get the coin?" Dresden asked.

Da's face twisted. *"Yuldesh, hir isad."* Alright, my son. Da dropped to one knee and pulled Dresden to his chest, nearly strangling him in a tight embrace. Dresden buried his face in Da's shoulder as he clutched his father's shirt. *"Yuldesh, hir lodde tam,"* Da murmured. *Alright, my brave boy.*

They tied up the cow and goat and followed Harreldon into the tavern, through a crowded room that smelled of pipe smoke, up rickety stairs into a tiny room with a sagging cot and table hardly big enough for Harreldon to lay out what he explained was the contract of indenture. Da signed his name with an X, and Dresden clumsily wrote his own name under the lines of Monparthian text he couldn't read. Harreldon handed Da a bulging sack of coin and looked at Dresden.

"Let's go. I want to leave this disgusting place."

Da made a strange noise in his throat. "Right now?"

Harreldon waved the parchment. "Yes, now. His life is not his own. Assuming he doesn't do anything to increase his debt, he'll be his own man again in ten years."

Dresden wiped his sweaty hands on his ratty trousers. Ten years was so long.

"Can...can I send him something?" Da asked, his voice strained. "To the Kimberly castle?"

The man shrugged. "So long as his master allows him to keep it."

Da nodded and hugged Dresden again. "I'll bring you your scimitars," he whispered in Carasian. "I'm sorry, Dresden. This shouldn't be your burden to bear. You're too young..." Da shook his head and firmly patted Dresden's back. "Do well. Serve well. Stay out of trouble. Make us proud. May Etiros protect you and keep you."

The final goodbyes were a blur. Harreldon mounted a horse and pulled Dresden up behind him. Dresden clutched Harreldon's belt as he watched Da fade away into the distance. *What have I done?*

EYES DOWN

The same day

Dresden's mouth fell open as they approached the castle. He'd never gone near it before. It was so big, with its towering gray stone wall and central stone tower. Several multi-story wood buildings that looked far more solid than the ones in town flanked the tower. They stopped in the courtyard, empty except for a few servants going about their tasks. Harreldon dismounted and lifted Dresden down.

"I'm going to present you to Lord Kimberly and Master Hargreaves," Harreldon said gruffly. "Bow when you see them. Keep your eyes lowered, don't speak unless you are asked a question, if you must answer a question, refer to Lord Kimberly as my lord and Master Hargreaves as master. To be clear for the future, you will call Lady Kimberly my lady, and everyone else mistress or master. Understood?"

Dresden nodded, unable to speak. Harrledon escorted him inside. Dresden gawked as they walked down a hallway covered with a crimson carpet, past vases and carved busts on pedestals. Harreldon ushered him into a side room with plush armchairs.

"Wait here. Don't touch anything. Just…stand still." Harreldon slipped out of the door.

Dresden stood stiffly and studied the paintings on the walls. Some kind of serpent with icy-blue scales and spikes around its face in a snowstorm. A giant cat that had tusks like a boar, prowling toward a deer. He shuddered and stared at the ground.

My lord, master. My lord, master. As the moments ticked by, he wondered what his master would be like. Would he be kind? Cruel? *Etiros, let him be kind.*

The door creaked open. Harreldon looked at Dresden with distaste. "This way, Jakobs."

He led Dresden into another little room, this one with smaller cushioned chairs arranged in a semicircle. A brown-haired man wearing clothes that looked even finer than Harreldon's sat in one of the chairs, his muscular build lounging casually. He wore a bored expression. *Must be Lord Kimberly.*

A boy with a round, earnest face stood near the man, but not too near. He'd left a healthy gap between himself and Lord Kimberly. Black hair curled around his ears and over his pale forehead. His light gray eyes fixed on Dresden, his expression curious. In contrast to the vivid dyes and layers of Lord Kimberly's clothing, the boy wore only a simple navy tunic with a plain black belt and gray trousers.

They stopped in the middle of the room, and Dresden did his best bow. Lord Kimberly snorted, and Dresden hoped his face wasn't as red as it felt.

"Lord Kimberly, Master Hargreaves," Harreldon said with a bow. "This is Dresden Jakobs." He handed the boy a rolled-up parchment. "That's the signed indenture."

Master Hargreaves tucked the parchment into his belt.

"He's foreign," Kimberly said.

"He speaks Monparthian fine." Harreldon shrugged.

Kimberly's upper lip curled. "And he's a mess. You'll have to get him cleaned up, Hargreaves, I won't have some peasant running about my estate looking like a beggar."

"Of course, my lord," Hargreaves said quietly.

"And you're responsible for him. Make sure he knows how to behave. I can't imagine he knows anything, so you'll have to make sure he knows his duties and doesn't cause trouble." Kimberly drummed his fingers on the arm of his chair.

"I will."

Kimberly glared at Hargreaves, and the boy flinched.

"I will, my lord."

Dresden's forehead wrinkled. *That seems odd.*

"What are you gawking at?" Kimberly snapped. Dresden quickly bowed his head. "Discipline might be a problem," Kimberly mused. "You might want to purchase a whip."

Dresden's hands went cold. *What?*

"A—a whip, my lord?" Hargreaves stuttered. "He's not a horse or a slave."

"He's indentured, he might as well be a slave." Kimberly sniffed. "Besides, foreign servants are always troublesome."

Terror coiled around Dresden's chest and squeezed. *A...slave?* His knees wobbled. *Da was right. I was foolish. I can't do this.* His gaze flicked to the contract in Hargreaves' belt, and he remembered what Harreldon had said about being hunted. *I have to. I'm trapped.* Understanding of his situation crashed over him. He was entirely at the mercy of this boy and Lord Kimberly.

You're doing this for Tatya and Ma. But even that thought couldn't stop the fear gnawing at his stomach. Fear that soured and turned into resentment toward his new master.

Kimberly stood. "I better write my cousin and tell him I did as requested and got his mistake a servant." Hargreaves' shoulders inched toward his ears. Kimberly strode out, and Harreldon followed. The moment the door closed, Hargreaves' entire body relaxed.

"Hello." Hargreaves smiled. It was a kind, open smile. The kind of smile Dresden would take as an invitation to be friends from one of the village boys. *Keep your eyes down.* Dresden lowered his gaze.

"Hello, master."

"Oh, please, don't do that." Hargreaves cleared his throat. "I mean, in front of Kimberly, probably do. He'll expect it. But...you can call me Regulus the rest of the time."

Dresden's gaze snapped up. "Master Regulus?"

"I suppose that works." Regulus sighed. "Come on. I'll show you around."

Dresden followed him out of the room. He didn't trust his new master's friendliness. Nobles were supposed to be self-obsessed, dismissive of their servants. But...

Could they be friends?

Kimberly's mention of a whip made him shudder. *No, I won't trust him. Not when he's getting a whip to use on me.*

Dresden felt numb as Regulus lead him through the castle, explaining where things were. They ended the tour at Regulus' small room. Dresden had a tiny side room attached to Regulus', just big enough for small cot and a chamber pot. That night, he cried himself to sleep.

DROWN

Age: 10
Location: Kimberly Estate, Monparth

When Da brought Dresden his scimitars a week later, Regulus let them go for a walk together. Da told him how well they were doing with the extra silver and no longer owing any coin. It made the ache in Dresden's chest dull a little. When Regulus caught Dresden trying to hide the scimitars in his room, he told him not to worry about it. In fact, he'd been fascinated and begged Dresden to tell him about them. He let Dresden keep the blades in his room. And as far as Dresden knew, Regulus didn't buy a whip.

Still, Dresden didn't trust him. Kimberly and his son, Hendrick, were mocking and cruel, to both Regulus and Dresden. Dresden didn't imagine Regulus could be around that and not become equally malicious. But every time Dresden got in trouble for not looking humble enough, or being in the wrong place, or speaking out of turn, Regulus defended him.

"I don't care how you act when Kimberly and Hendrick aren't around," Regulus said one day. "But please, keep your eyes down and don't talk unless you have to around them. Someday, I might not be able to stop them."

Of course, that was easier said than done. Servants

were supposed to be quiet, unobtrusive, to stand still and not gawk. Dresden quickly grew restless. Being a servant was harder than anticipated.

But he didn't know what to make of the genuine concern in his master's eyes. *I can't trust him. He's one of them.* But he wasn't—not really. The other servants told Dresden that Regulus was the illegitimate son of Lord Arrano, Lord Kimberly's distant cousin. Kimberly barely tolerated Regulus. The more time Dresden spent around them, the more he hated how the Kimberlys treated Regulus. Except for Brigid Kimberly, who was the same age as Dresden. She sometimes teased Regulus, but not in the malicious way Hendrick did.

Still, Dresden wouldn't get his hopes up that Regulus truly cared about him.

One morning three months into his indenture, they went for Regulus' morning run. He always had Dresden come along. Dresden kept a respectful distance behind Regulus, despite Regulus trying to get him to run alongside him.

As they neared the river that cut across Kimberly's fields, the morning mist thickened, and the sound of rushing water filled his ears. Dresden tensed. He didn't like crossing the narrow wooden bridge over the river, especially when the river was swollen and rushing from recent heavy rainfall. He'd never learned to swim, and the railing-less bridge terrified him, but he wouldn't let Regulus know his weakness.

Fog swirled over the river and clouded the banks. Regulus ran across, his longer legs stretching effortlessly as Dresden struggled to keep up. A twinge went through his side as he neared the center of the bridge.

His steps wavered, and his foot caught on a part of the bridge slick with morning dew. He twisted and fell, his feet plunging into freezing water. He clawed at the edge of the slippery, worn wood as the current tugged on his feet. With a scream, he fell, and the river dragged him under.

Dresden thrashed, darkness swirling around him. *Which way is up?* His heart hammered. He kicked as his lungs constricted, making it harder to hold his breath. His head broke water, and he tried to breathe, but got a mouthful of water as he sank back under. He sputtered, only drawing in more water through his nose and mouth. He flailed about looking for something, anything to grab onto. His hand hit something, and he tried to grab it, but it shifted. Something tugged on his arm.

He struck out, trying to free himself from whatever was pulling him down. Somehow, he managed to get his head above water. He blinked stinging water from his eyes as he coughed and gasped, his lungs burning, and continued to fight the river. Something tightened around his chest. He kicked and thrashed.

"Dresden! Stop fighting me!"

Regulus' voice cut through his fuzzy thoughts. He whipped his head around. Regulus' face was inches from his, strained with concentration.

"Calm down so I can swim!"

Dresden forced his trembling limbs to stop flailing. Regulus pulled Dresden's back closer against his chest and dragged him toward the bank, his legs bumping into Dresden's as he kicked. Dresden coughed up water that burned his throat and nose. Regulus pushed him up onto the bank, then climbed up and dragged him away from the river's edge. Dresden rolled onto his side and vomited water. He gulped down air, shivering from the cold.

"Dresden!" Regulus seized his shoulders and searched his face, his eyes wide. "Are you alright?"

Dresden nodded wearily and tried to speak, but his voice came out in a croak. He cleared his throat. "Fine. I'm fine."

"Blessed Etiros above, Dresden. You scared me! You can't swim?"

"No." He coughed again and scrunched his shoulders.

"Well, I'll teach you." Regulus laid back on the grass, his chest heaving. "I'm glad you're alright."

Dresden shivered again. "You...saved me."

Regulus threw his arm over his eyes, hiding the top half of his face. "I was afraid I wasn't going to reach you in time."

"Why did you save me?" Dresden looked at him warily.

"Why?" Regulus removed his arm from over his eyes and frowned. "Someone needs help, and you can help, you help them. And you're my only friend."

"Friend?"

Regulus sighed and sat up. "Look, I know—good gracious, you're shaking. Come on." He pulled Dresden to his feet and led him back to his room, where he forced Dresden to dress in dry clothes. As Dresden dressed, Regulus stoked the fire.

"That's my job, master—"

"I saved your life, maybe you can just call me Regulus now." Regulus added another log to the fire, still wearing his own soaking clothes. He only changed once Dresden was settled in Regulus' single armchair in front of the fire, wrapped in one of Regulus' thick, soft blankets.

"Thank you...Regulus." Dresden clutched the blanket around his shoulders.

Regulus grinned as he peeled off his wet clothes. "I'd hoped we could be friends. I don't really need a servant. All my fath—" He winced. "Lord Arrano's idea. But a friend? I'd like to have a friend."

"You're not like the Kimberlys at all."

Regulus drew back as if slapped. "I hope not. Is that why you've been distant? You thought I was like them?"

Dresden flushed. "You kind of bought me. That's what the other servants say. I was afraid you'd become like them, or that you were pretending to be nice."

Regulus pulled on dry clothes and sat on the floor next to the armchair, his chin cupped his hand. "I'm sorry. I hadn't thought of it that way. You...agreed, though, didn't you?"

"Yes. My Da owed some bad men lots of silver." He shrugged. "Now Da doesn't have to sell the animals, and Tatya has two new dresses, and Da said he is going to replace the doors with ones the wind can't get through."

Regulus looked up at him. "Who's Tatya?"

"My little sister."

"Oh." Regulus' face fell. He looked at the fire. "I'm sorry you had to leave your family. I guess it makes sense you don't want to be my friend."

Dresden sank deeper into Regulus' armchair. "Maybe...we could be friends."

Regulus straightened. "Really? I've never had a

21

friend." His face went crimson and he looked away.

"I guess you have one now." Dresden smiled.

Thank you for letting him be nice, Etiros.

Trouble

Age: 13
Location: Kimberly Estate, Lanure Duchy, Monparth

"I was only following my lady's orders." Dresden lifted his chin and glared at Hendrick. Morning sunlight shone through the branches of one of the many trees in the walled-in garden next to Lord Kimberly's castle, making him squint. Not really the unafraid look he had hoped would hide his inner dread.

Hendrick was older, taller, and more muscular. Not to mention a lord's son. At thirteen, Dresden was a scrappy servant. The smart thing would be to grovel and beg forgiveness. But Dresden had never been particularly good at groveling, and he'd done nothing wrong. Well, nothing terribly wrong.

"Really, Hendrick." Brigid tugged on her older brother's sleeve. Her silky chestnut hair was wound in braids above her round, pale face and wide eyes. She was short, even for a thirteen-year-old girl. Which was why she'd asked for Dresden's help. "I told him to—"

"Go inside, Brigid." Hendrick gently but firmly pushed her away. "The servant boy should have known better, so he's either a cad or an idiot."

Dresden glowered and forced his hands not to curl into fists.

"Either way, a beating should get through your thick Carasian skull."

Dresden didn't even have time to get angry at Hendrick for using his foreign heritage as an insult, because Hendrick was already pulling his fist back. Again, the smart thing to do would be to stand still and take it. But instinct took over, and Dresden reflexively raised his hands to shield his face. He squeezed his eyes shut as he realized the beating would likely be worse for trying to thwart it.

The blow didn't land.

There was a sharp smack and someone grunted, but it wasn't Dresden. Dresden opened his eyes to a head of thick black hair.

"Move, bastard," Hendrick growled. "That blow wasn't meant for you, but this one will be if you don't get out of my way."

Regulus didn't move, still shielding Dresden with his body. "Dresden is my servant. Any discipline he may need falls to me. We've discussed this." Regulus' voice was steady as he looked up at his cousin. He was barely fourteen but already tall, only a few inches shorter than seventeen-year-old Hendrick. "Now. What happened?"

"He put his hands on Brigid." Hendrick glared at Dresden over Regulus' shoulder.

The disappointment in Regulus' sigh stung far worse than Hendrick's insults. "My lady Brigid, is that true?"

Brigid glanced at her brother uncertainly. "I wanted to see over the wall to watch the horses. Dresden was just helping me balance on the back of the bench. I asked him to."

"And he should have refused!" Hendrick crossed his

arms. "Good thing I happened by, because your filthy servant had his hands on my sister's waist."

Dresden winced. Okay, he hadn't thought it through. He should have said no. Or at least only held her hand. But it had felt natural to support her by her waist. And then maybe he did stand a bit closer than he should have...she was really pretty.

Regulus shifted and turned slightly so he could see Dresden without turning his back on his cousin. "Jakobs. Do you understand what you did was wrong?"

Dresden lowered his head. "Yes, master."

"Then what do you do?"

Dresden sighed and bent low toward Hendrick. "I made a mistake. It should not have happened, and I swear, it will not happen again. I humbly beg your forgiveness, Master Kimberly, Mistress Kimberly." Ugh, groveling. He'd find a way not to be a servant one day. He'd earn enough to buy a freeman's holding far from any pompous nobles.

"Your servant is presumptuous and has an attitude problem," Hendrick said coldly. "He needs a beating. If you won't do it, I will."

"Wait." Regulus blocked Dresden from Hendrick. "He's useless to me beaten. I'll deny his next meals—"

"You're soft, Hargreaves," a new male voice intruded.

Dresden glanced up, still bowed, his hands going cold at Lord Kimberly's voice. Regulus offered a quick, stiff bow to his father's cousin as Lord Kimberly approached. Kimberly always looked severe, with his lean, muscular frame and heavy brow. But the disapproving scowl slashed across his mouth made him look more unapproachable than usual.

"Hendrick is correct. Your servant overstepped his station. You must learn to control him, or he will continue to be a rotten servant."

I'm not a rotten servant. Indignation rippled through Dresden, but he kept his head respectfully bowed as he watched the others through his lashes. *I do my job.*

"Yes, my lord." Regulus inclined his head. "I will speak—"

"Speak?" Lord Kimberly's eyes narrowed. "He's your servant. You don't reason with him; you punish his wrongdoing."

"My lord..." Regulus swallowed audibly. "It was a mistake."

"And when he's been properly punished, he will make fewer mistakes." Lord Kimberly turned his cold eyes on Dresden. "Take off your belt, boy, and give it to your master."

Brigid gasped. "Father—"

"Go inside, Brigid." Kimberly, as usual, would allow no argument. Brigid fled the garden, her pink dress rustling as she ran. "Now, boy."

Dresden's hands shook, but he complied. He kept his eyes on the ground as he offered the belt to Regulus. He supposed three years as an indentured servant without a single beating was more than he could have hoped for. Regulus did not take it.

"My lord, please." Regulus' voice had lost its confidence. "It was a first offence."

Hendrick snorted. "Your servant often offends, he just does it differently every time. And you allow it, *Reg.*"

Dresden winced. So, Hendrick had overheard them. He knew that Regulus let Dresden call him Regulus, or even Reg, instead of *master*. At least, when they thought no one was listening.

"He is my servant," Regulus said with a shrug. "No one else calls me master, and my name is more respectful than bastard."

There was a terrible moment of silence. Regulus had gone too far, Dresden was certain.

Kimberly sighed. "Hargreaves, Lord Arrano saw fit to give you a servant. If you don't discipline him properly, you do my cousin further discredit. Now take the belt and punish your wayward servant."

Further. Because to some, Regulus' existence did his father discredit. Kimberly refused to even refer to Lord Arrano as Regulus' father, and wouldn't let Regulus do so, either. *I may be foreign and a servant, but at least no one thinks I shouldn't have been born.*

Regulus took a deep, slow breath. He took the belt. Dresden tried not to let his fear or resentment show as he turned and stepped over to brace himself against a nearby oak. He should have known better than to hope his master could be a true friend, even if he was kind.

"My lord, you are right," Regulus said slowly. "The fault is with me, not Jakobs. I have not kept a close enough eye on him or disciplined him enough. His failure as a servant is merely a reflection of my failure as a master. A dog cannot be blamed for stealing from the table if his master feeds him scraps. I will do better in the future. But for now, the problem is me, and the just punishment should be mine."

Dresden's breath caught. He looked over his shoulder. Regulus held the belt out to Kimberly, his eyes downcast. Hendrick smirked. The corner of Kimberly's mouth twitched. He wouldn't—Kimberly took the belt.

"If that's what you want, Hargreaves."

Dresden nearly choked. "Master—"

"Step aside, Jakobs." Regulus' spine was rigidly straight, but he wouldn't meet Dresden's eyes. "Now."

Dresden moved several steps aside, more out of fear of making things worse than any desire to watch Regulus be beaten. Regulus placed his hands on the oak trunk, bracing himself.

"You want your tunic ruined, bastard?" Hendrick taunted.

Regulus grimaced. "A wise consideration, cousin." He pulled off his loose tunic and tossed it to Dresden. Dresden caught it, staring dumbly at Regulus' bare back. He looked frightfully pale compared to Dresden's rich, dark olive skin. Pale and exposed. The shirt was unlikely to have been ruined. But it might have softened the blows. Regulus braced himself against the tree again.

"What's this?" Kimberly stepped forward and hooked his finger on the thin leather cord around Regulus' neck and drew it back. Regulus clutched the necklace in his fist.

"It's mine. From my father—I mean Lord Arrano."

Kimberly stilled. "What is it?"

Regulus' shoulders shook. "A ring." Why he should be afraid of showing the ring, Dresden didn't know. He'd thought Regulus kept it always on his person for safe-keeping.

Kimberly's face darkened. He dropped his hand. "Show me."

Regulus turned from the tree, his expression drawn. Slowly he eased his fist and lowered his hand. Kimberly snatched up the ring, the cord taut against Regulus' neck.

"He gave you this, boy?"

"I swear it." Regulus' lower lip trembled. "Before I left. He said to keep it in case I ever had need of it, but to keep it secret. Not to tell a soul. I know I shouldn't have it, but he gave it to me. I didn't steal it, and I don't intend to use it, my lord. Just keep it."

Dresden looked between Regulus and Kimberly, uncomprehending. He'd never looked closely at the tarnished silver ring. Kimberly let the ring fall back to Regulus' bare chest.

"My cousin is more of a fool than I thought." Kimberly looked furious. "That could cause trouble. Only an heir should carry a signet ring."

Dresden clutched Regulus' shirt in his clammy hands.

"I know, my lord." Regulus lowered his head. "I don't know why he gave it to me. But I've never shown it to anyone."

"Never speak of it again." Kimberly stepped back. "Turn around! Let's get this over with."

Regulus' hands had barely touched the bark when Kimberly drew his hand back. The belt whirred through the air and slapped loudly against Regulus' skin. Regulus twitched and his hands curled against the trunk, but he didn't make a sound. A red line blazed across Regulus' back. As Kimberly drew back again, Dresden squeezed his eyes shut. *Whir. Smack. Whir. Smack.* Again, and again. Regulus cried out. Dresden opened his eyes, afraid to see the aftermath. But Kimberly wasn't done. *Whir. Smack.* Regulus sagged against the tree and whimpered. Again Lord Kimberly pulled back, and it took every ounce of Dresden's resolve not to interfere. It would only make things worse.

The belt hit and Regulus screamed; his knees buckled. Tears squeezed from Dresden's eyes as Kimberly hit Regulus again and Regulus cried, leaning against the tree on his knees.

Kimberly looked at Dresden. "I hope that taught you a lesson as well, boy." He threw the belt at Dresden, and Dresden fumbled it, dropping it and Regulus' shirt to the stone garden path. Hendrick snickered.

"Get up, Hargreaves," Kimberly said with a sigh.

Regulus whimpered and his body trembled, but he pulled himself up on the tree and turned toward his guardian. He managed a small bow, his face pinched with pain. "Thank you, my lord. I will do better."

Kimberly grunted. "You better. I'd hate to have to tell Lord Arrano his mistake can longer reside here. Remember, Hargreaves. You're lucky. Things could be worse. So make the most of your situation, and don't abuse my hospitality by allowing your servant to subvert his station. And keep that signet ring hidden."

"Yes, my lord," Regulus said quietly. "I'm grateful for your kindness."

Kindness? Dresden clutched the shirt and belt. *He just beat you!*

Kimberly nodded, then turned away. Hendrick followed his father out of the garden, and Dresden rushed to Regulus' side.

"Reg," he whispered. "What the hell were you thinking?"

"I couldn't do it." Regulus reached for his shirt and

grimaced. He spoke so softly Dresden barely heard him. "I wouldn't hurt my only friend."

Guilt twisted Dresden's stomach. "I'm sorry. If I hadn't been stupid—"

"It's in the past." Regulus pulled on his shirt with a stifled cry. "Go ask Luke for some salve. Say it was a training accident. I'll meet you in my room."

Dresden got the salve as quickly as he could. Regulus was sitting slumped over the back of a chair, his shirt tossed aside. The red lines crisscrossing his back were dotted with dark blue bruises, and pinpricks of crimson showed where the belt had split his skin. Dresden immediately began slathering the lines with the pungent salve, praying to Etiros it would somehow help.

"I can't believe..." He shook his head.

Regulus chuckled drily. "I think he's wanted to do that for some time. He just didn't have a good excuse." He flinched as Dresden touched his back again. "I'm an embarrassment to have around. As if my disgrace taints them. He keeps me for my father's coin. Both the money my father sends for the inconvenience of raising me, and the part of my allowance I know he keeps."

Dresden shifted uncomfortably. Regulus had never talked about his situation. He always bore the insults from Hendrick and the thinly veiled jabs from Lord Kimberly without comment, even in private, and Dresden had never dared to broach the subject.

"But...it's not your fault," Dresden said.

"I know that!" Regulus jerked. "Etiros above, don't tell me things I already know!" He shoved out of the chair. "I didn't ask to be born, or to be sent here! I am polite, I stay out of trouble, I train hard to earn my knighthood so I can leave! But it's never good enough! I'm never good enough."

Regulus leaned on the table, his shoulders trembling. The salve glistened over the dark red lines from the beating that should have been Dresden's. Dresden clutched the little clay jar, unsure what to do as shame gnawed at his skin.

"And now..." Regulus' head sank lower. He looked so young and lonely. "The bastard and his servant friend. You know what they'll say? I'm too comfortable with you because I should be you. They'll say I know deep down I'm more my mother's son than my father's. Maybe they're right."

Dresden stared at the jar. He should apologize for making Regulus' life worse. But for the first time in years, he was afraid of how Regulus might react to him.

"Lord Kimberly and Hendrick will be watching more closely." Regulus sniffed, his voice hoarse. "We're going to need to be more formal. Even in private, so we don't slip up. Master and Jakobs. Understood?"

A hollow ache settled in Dresden's chest. "Yes, master."

He tried to tell himself it was worse for Regulus. At least the other servants were friendly. Regulus had no other friends. But it felt like Dresden was being punished; pushed down to his station, as Kimberly said.

Regulus took a deep breath. "Good." He moved back to the chair. "Finish, ple—" He grunted. "Too friendly," he muttered under his breath. "Finish, Jakobs."

"Yes, master." Dresden returned to applying the

salve as anger fought his guilt. "I'm sorry. I won't get you in trouble again."

Regulus flinched as Dresden's fingers brushed a bit of ripped skin. Dresden finished and stepped away. Regulus remained slumped over the back of the chair, letting the salve dry. With nothing else to do and unable to stare any longer at the bruises, Dresden set about tidying up Regulus' small room. Not that there was much to clean. Regulus didn't own much. But the desk could use dusting.

"Drez," Regulus said softly.

Dresden looked up from arranging a stack of books on warfare. Was the use of the nickname to see if he would fail to remember his new instructions? "Yes, master?"

"It won't be forever." It was hard to hear Regulus, he spoke so quietly, with his forehead resting on his arm on the back of the chair. "When I'm knighted, my father will allow me back. I'm sure of it. And if not, we can travel. Find another lord I can pledge to, who won't care who I call my friend."

Dresden wasn't sure how to respond to that.

Regulus sighed. "Just...don't hate me, Drez— Jakobs." He sniffed and wiped at his face. "Please don't hate me."

"You took a beating for me." He stared at Regulus' welted back. "I don't think I could hate you, Reg— master."

"Good." Regulus stood with a grunt and moved to his bed. As he carefully laid on his stomach, Dresden heard him mutter, "I need one person who doesn't hate me."

THE RIVER

Age: 16
Location: Kimberly Estate, Lanure Duchy, Monparth

"Okay, first of all, that was a dirty and underhanded move, and you know it." Regulus shoved Dresden's shoulder hard enough to make Dresden stagger a step sideways, but he was grinning. Sweat glistened on Regulus' face and stuck in his patchy stubble. It was a constant source of disappointment to Regulus that, at seventeen, he could barely manage a decent layer of stubble, while Dresden's beard was already thick at sixteen.

They both stank from their afternoon of training. Training in the heat of the day was awful, but Hendrick and his friends avoided the training yard when the sun was hottest, providing Regulus and Dresden a chance to train unbothered.

"No, see, there's no such thing as a dirty and underhanded move in a fight." Dresden would have pushed Regulus right back, but they couldn't risk someone seeing him appear to attack his master.

Kimberly castle towered not far behind them as they walked across the field at the rear of the castle. Any guard on patrol or servant going about their tasks or even one of the Kimberlys could see them, and Kimberly seemed to always be waiting for another chance to humiliate or hurt Regulus. Thankfully, Regulus was good at denying Kimberly any openings, and Dresden had learned to do the same.

"Hmmm, sounds like something a cheater would say." Regulus laughed. "Admit it, you cheated, Jakobs."

"Yes, master."

Regulus flinched. "Not like that," he whispered. "It wasn't an order."

Dresden's face heated. Over the last three years, the response had become rote. Regulus said Jakobs, Dresden said yes, master. Or, on occasion, no, master. They still blurred the lines between servant and friend, more so as the belting became a distant memory, but Regulus strictly enforced the Jakobs/master rule of address. It *did* help deter Kimberly's wrath. And had become so normal, it didn't bother Dresden anymore. Most of the time. If he didn't dwell on it.

"Well, then, no, I didn't cheat. My father said, if you're fighting to survive, you do what you have to in order to live. Anything is fair in war, so there's no such thing as cheating in a fight."

Regulus chuckled. "Your father is a philosophical farmer."

"No, he's a practical one." Dresden shrugged. "My parents grew up in a borderland in Carasom, between feuding warlords. Dangerous area, everyone knew how to fight to protect their family. That's why they moved to Monparth. And why he started training me with the scimitars at six, as his father trained him."

"Hm." Regulus' expression sobered. "In such a situation, when you're fighting to protect your family..." He nodded. "You do what you must to survive and save others. Protecting those you care about is more important than your personal honor."

Regulus frowned, his brows pinching as he looked lost in thought. Dresden wondered if he was thinking about that awful belting. Regulus shook his head and smiled.

"But, when it's not a matter of life and death, honor matters, which is why I'm giving you three seconds' head start to the river."

Dresden scowled. "Now that's insult—"

"Go! One—"

Dresden took off at a run, grinning over his shoulder as Regulus counted off two and three and followed. A stitch in his side developed almost immediately, his aching body protesting running after three hours of sword practice. He pushed past the pain, determined to win this time as he leapt over a low dry-stone wall and skirted a bush. The sound of his own labored breathing filled his ears. He wound through a grove of trees. The wide and deep bend of the river came into view across the grassy pasture. A couple cows were drinking on the far side. Poor things were going to have quite a fright. Dresden leaned forward, fighting his burning calves and the pinching in his side.

"So close," Regulus shouted as he sped past.

Dresden tried to catch up, but Regulus' legs were too accursedly long. Regulus leapt into the river with a terrific splash. The cows lowed and skittered. Dresden leapt into the river. The water was startlingly cold, and he resurfaced with a yell.

"Nope!" Regulus wrapped his arm around Dresden's shoulders, wrestling him back under. "Losers get submerged!"

Dresden dunked under and broke out of Regulus' grip. He burst back up and splashed Regulus, laughing. "Unchivalrous!"

"Says the man who kicked up dirt in my face!" Regulus laughed, a wide grin on his face as he jumped on Dresden's back and pushed him back under.

Dresden grabbed Regulus' shirt and pulled him under, then climbed up Regulus until he was sitting on his shoulders. "You're a sorry loser."

"You're a sorry runner." Regulus pushed Dresden off his shoulders, sending him tumbling back into the water with a splash.

Dresden came up sputtering and found Regulus leisurely floating on his back. "You have an unfair advantage, and you know it." Dresden splashed Regulus' face, and Regulus blinked rapidly. "You want to grow up to be a troll or something? You done growing yet?"

"I gave you a head start." Regulus ducked under, and when he came back up, he spit a stream of water into Dresden's face.

"Ugh, charming." Dresden wiped off his face but couldn't stop smiling. Times like this, hidden from view from the castle, just for a moment, they weren't master and servant. They were friends. As much as a master and servant could be friends.

"What do you think," a light female voice said, "if we ask, will they take off their shirts?"

They spun toward the bank they'd leapt from. Lady Brigid, looking like a dream in a pale blue dress that hugged her curves and bared her shoulders, stood near the bank. Her brown hair fell in soft waves down her back. One of her friends was with her. Lady Margaret's ginger hair was half up in intricate braids and she wore a peach-colored gown with a maroon belt that accentuated her waist. One of Lady Brigid's handmaids, her black tresses tied back in a bun, trailed behind them. *Kiara.* Dresden sent a smile Kiara's way as his thoughts wandered to a lovely night a few weeks ago, involving a bonfire and a stolen kiss...

"I think if we ordered Jakobs to, he'd have to obey us, wouldn't he?" Brigid grinned wickedly, her eyes sparkling.

"That seems right to me." Margaret laughed. "Take off your shirt, Jakobs."

Dresden flushed and looked helplessly to Regulus. Regulus looked unamused, but then a relaxed smile slid over his features.

"Ladies, my servant need only obey me. But more importantly, it is my duty to ensure your innocence is protected."

Brigid's smile twitched like she was trying not to laugh. "Come, Regulus. As soaked as you are, we won't be seeing that much more."

"We did walk all the way out here." Margaret winked. "And not to see cows."

"Um..." Regulus cleared his throat. "Pardon?"

"I know you often come here after training." Brigid's smile turned teasing.

Dresden mentally cursed. If the ladies knew of their swimming routine, Hendrick might as well. Regulus would realize this, and insist they act more formal and distanced.

"And"—Brigid blushed—"we can't get a good look at you in the training yard."

Dresden's face burned so hot he wanted nothing more than to duck under the water. He glanced over at Regulus. Regulus had turned cherry red.

"Such admissions are inappropriate," Regulus said quietly.

"Oh, stop being so chivalrous." Margaret stepped closer. "You'd be more comfortable with your shirts off instead of weighing you down with all that water, wouldn't you?"

Dresden glanced at Kiara. She was blushing, but also looked like she was trying not to laugh...and a little eager. Well, if that's what it took to get another kiss... He looked at Regulus, waiting for some indication of what to do. Regulus looked as uncertain as Dresden felt.

Brigid stepped close to the bank. "Oh, it's just some harmless fun!"

"My lady," Regulus' voice was firm, "your father would not approve."

"Please." Margaret rolled her eyes. "Scared of Lord Kimberly, Master Hargreaves?" She fluttered her eyes at Regulus.

Brigid's smile faltered. Regulus lowered his head, not looking at the girls. Dresden could practically hear the echo of the belt slapping against Regulus' back.

Brigid took Margaret's arm. "Let's leave them be."

"What?" Margaret frowned. "But—"

"Let's go, Margaret!" Brigid pulled Margaret away.

Kiara stalled, still standing near the riverbank. She looked at the retreating ladies as Dresden flopped back to float on the calm surface, feeling relieved but also a little disappointed to be denied the chance to show off. Kiara looked back at them.

"I have to admit, I'm disappointed. I was curious, Master Hargreaves."

Regulus made an odd squeaking noise.

"What, not me?" Dresden straightened to stare at Kiara, offended.

Kiara grinned, her eyes twinkling with mischief. "Oh, that's a sight I've already managed to glimpse." Her smile turned seductive. "Not that I'm uninterested in taking a closer look." She spun away and hurried after the ladies.

Dresden gaped at her back. *Wait...what? When?*

Uproarious laughter invaded his thoughts. Regulus splashed him. "She *likes* you! I wonder if it was all her idea." Regulus splashed him again. "What's her name?"

"Kiara," Dresden mumbled.

"Kiara." Regulus laughed. "As awkward as that was—especially now that every time I see Brigid and Margaret, I'm going to be self-conscious—this is wonderful. Now I can tease you about *Kiara*."

"Tease away." Dresden pushed Regulus over. "I already kissed her."

"You *what*?" Regulus chuckled and pushed him back. "Scoundrel!"

Dresden grinned. "I'm pretty sure Lady Margaret would gladly kiss you—"

"Shut up." Regulus shoved Dresden under.

"—if you're interested," Dresden finished as he popped back up.

"One year, and we're free. I'm not risking that by kissing a pretty girl." Regulus made little waves with his arms, staring at the ripples.

"So you admit she's pretty? Because she definitely thinks you're handsome."

Regulus scowled and splashed him again, but amusement showed in his eyes. "Come on. We need to get cleaned up before supper."

They moved to the bank, but as Dresden started to climb up, Regulus grabbed his shirt and yanked him back into the river. When he resurfaced, Regulus was standing on the bank grinning while squeezing excess water out of his shirt. "What are you still splashing around for?"

Dresden rolled his eyes and clambered onto the bank. "I've half a mind to push you back in and make a run for it."

"Bad plan." Regulus shook his head, his expression serious as water sprayed from his hair. "You run too slowly for that."

"Rude. You'll see. I'll win one of these days."

"Sure. The same day you beat me without scimitars or cheating." Regulus headed back toward the castle, and Dresden followed.

He wouldn't admit it, but he knew he couldn't defeat Regulus with a broadsword. He could barely hold his own against him with his scimitars, and they were lighter, faster weapons and had the advantage of two blades to one. Which was why Regulus loved fighting Dresden when he used the scimitars. He said it was a better challenge.

"I am sorry about getting dirt in your eyes."

Regulus chuckled. "Only be sorry that I'm not afraid to use that move on you now."

Dresden sighed. *Oh. Great.*

"Oh," Regulus said, "Lady Margaret being here likely means Lord Hatan is here, too, so I won't be able to sneak off from supper early. You'll have a little extra free time. You know, if you wanted to see if Kiara still wants to see your muscled chest."

"Shut up." Dresden quickly glanced around, hoping no one had heard him silence his master. No one seemed to be around as they walked into the castle's shadow.

"But I'll need these clothes cleaned and hung out to dry first, Jakobs."

"Yes, master." He smiled as they went in the servant's entrance so as not to drip water in the halls, and started making plans to pick some flowers before paying a visit to Kiara.

LET'S BE MERCENARIES

Age: 17
Location: Kimberly Estate, Lanure Duchy, Monparth

Dresden watched silently as Regulus paced back and forth, his long legs carrying him the length of his small room in a couple strides. He wondered again how tall Regulus' parents were. Lord Arrano had to be taller than his cousin Lord Kimberly, since Regulus had several inches on both Kimberly and Hendrick. Regulus kept muttering curses under his breath, his expression flickering between frightened and outraged. He stopped abruptly and turned on Dresden.

"Pack my things. Essentials only. Some clothes, my weapons. Get some food from the kitchen. I'm leaving."

Dresden gawked. Sure, someone hadn't just tried to murder Dresden, and the attempt on Regulus' life had shaken him, too. Still, leaving a week before Regulus' knighting ceremony seemed rash. "But—"

"Did I ask for your opinion or give an order?" Regulus sat at his desk, his movements hard and furious as he searched through a drawer. Dresden tried not to take the snapping personally. Regulus was kind, although sometimes he pretended to be harsh in front of the Kimberlys. But this was different. He was legitimately angry.

"Apologies, master." Dresden started up from the

chair and immediately began pulling clothes out of Regulus' small oak dresser.

Regulus sighed. "I'm sorry; I'm not upset with you, and that was uncalled for." He mussed his hair. "There's no point in staying. The Kimberlys don't want me here, and I don't want to stay here. I was a fool to think I could return to Arrano, that my father would want me once I was knighted, that Lady Arrano..." He growled. "I'll never be accepted by nobles who think I don't deserve to live. Even the knighthood won't change their minds when they find out what I am."

Dresden winced. "There are lords other than your family, who might—"

"I'm done trying to impress nobles." Regulus snatched up his quill. "I'm releasing you from your service; you're no longer indentured and are free to seek employment elsewhere. You'll get a week's worth of severance pay from my funds, assuming I can convince Lord Kimberly to release it to me instead of keeping it for himself."

"I...what?" Dresden froze and stared at Regulus. He worked his throat. "But...my contract was for ten years. I owe you three more years."

"And I have the right as the holder of your indenture to decide your extraordinary service has earned you an early release." Regulus finished writing something, then set the paper on the edge of the desk. "That reflects the terms of your indenture have been satisfied and you're a free man. I will write you a letter of recommendation." Regulus grabbed a blank sheet of parchment and scowled at the quill. "For whatever good it will do from an untitled bastard."

Dresden stared at the contract of indenture, his mind numb. *I'm...free? No longer bound as a servant?* He should say thank you. But he also wasn't sure he wanted to say goodbye to Regulus. "Where are you going?"

"I've heard of a mercenary troop that's currently passing through Lageness. I'm going to join them, if they'll take me." He glanced up, and something sparked in his gray eyes, his expression almost hopeful. "You could join me. Not as my servant, you're still released. But...as my friend." He glanced away.

"As...your friend?" Dresden stood rooted in place.

Regulus was his friend, no matter how distant they acted in public, and despite the respect Regulus demanded even in private as a precaution. Because when it came down to it, Regulus didn't treat him like a servant. He had been more worried about Dresden than himself in the immediate aftermath of the attack that morning. And over the years, Regulus had saved Dresden's hide on multiple occasions. Still, calling a friend "master" all the time and obeying his every order rankled, and could cause strain.

"Yes." Regulus paused in his writing and looked up, his brows creasing. "Unless...we aren't friends?" He swallowed hard and looked back down at the letter. "Which I would understand. You are free to take this letter and go as soon as I leave, if that's what you want." He dipped the quill again. "But I would miss you, Drez."

Drez. It had been years since Regulus had used the nickname. Dresden's mind spun. Mercenaries? They would be equals. And he could travel. Put his sword-fighting skills to good use. All those years of Regulus

47

filling their days with endless training could pay off. And they could be friends. Real friends, with no social constraints.

"Of course I'll go with you, Reg."

Regulus' head jerked up. "Are you sure?"

"Sounds like an adventure. Let's make a name for ourselves as mercenaries."

"Wait, then what am I writing this letter for?" Regulus grinned, his eyes crinkling, and stuck the quill back in the bottle of ink. "Better pack up your things, too. I have to go talk to Lord Kimberly. Be quick."

"Yes, master." Regulus frowned, and Dresden flushed. "Habit. I'll take care of it, Regulus."

Dresden had their packs ready with clothes and food by the time the door opened again some fifteen minutes later. Regulus' scowl could turn milk. A red mark covered his right cheek.

"Good, you're ready. Let's go." Regulus snatched his pack from Dresden and strode out. Dresden hurried after him.

"He struck you?"

Regulus grunted. "Apparently asking for my next month's allowance was impertinent. Better pray these mercenaries are looking to hire, because we're broke."

Dresden gulped and did send up a prayer, even though asking Etiros to help them get hired as mercenaries felt wrong.

The mercenary troop captain was a short and stocky man named Fletcher. Beady eyes watched them under a mess of greasy hair that shone in the firelight in the smoke-filled tavern. He sat back in his chair with his feet propped on a table. "Age?"

"Eighteen," Regulus said.

"Seventeen." Dresden shifted his pack on his back.

Fletcher grunted. "Bit young. No experience."

"Give us a chance to prove ourselves," Regulus said. "Hey, Kensen!"

A man nearly as tall as Regulus looked up from his tankard. His massive arms bulged under his discolored gray shirt, and scars that looked like claw marks ran down the side of his neck. "Aye, Captain?"

"These upstarts say they want to prove themselves. How's about a little duel?" The smile that split the captain's face was full of cruelty.

Kensen shrugged and walked over. "Sure, Captain." He eyed Regulus and Dresden. "One at a time, or both?"

The captain rubbed his chin, then pulled a coin out of the pouch at his belt. "Heads, both, tails, one at a time." He flipped the coin, caught it, and slapped it on the table. The king's crest rather than his profile stared up at them. He hooted. "One at a time!"

"I'll go first," Regulus said. He glanced at Dresden, and Dresden understood. Regulus was the better swordsman. If he was beaten, Dresden was free to back out.

They headed out, most of the other mercenaries coming to watch. The sun was sinking, and the air cooling rapidly. The captain claimed an empty livestock auction pen as a sparring ring, and Regulus and Kensen squared off. Dresden gripped the fence, every muscle tense.

Regulus was cautious at first, taking the defensive and avoiding as many blows as possible. He darted around the pen, his brow furrowed with concentration.

The mercenaries jeered and laughed. *Come on, Reg.* Regulus blocked a blow, tilted his head slightly. He blocked another. A flicker of a grin pulled at his mouth, then vanished. Dresden smiled.

"What are you smiling about, boy?" A lanky mercenary with several missing teeth laughed. "He's losing."

"Is he?"

Regulus parried a cut and switched to offensive in a blink. He stopped giving ground, pushing Kensen back with controlled, precise cuts and thrusts. The mercenaries quieted. Regulus kicked the mercenary in the gut, batted aside a poorly-aimed thrust, and put the tip of his sword to the man's throat. The mercenary dropped his sword.

Fletcher gaped at Regulus, then clapped. "You're hired. Your friend, too, I don't even care. If he's half as good as you, I'll be happy."

It took a moment for the reality to sink in. *We're mercenaries.*

CAUGHT SHIRKING

Age: 18
Location: Craigailte, near the Vaneltian border

Dresden slipped into the tent he shared with Regulus as quietly as possible. He'd been out far later than he'd realized, and he didn't want to wake his friend. He stole through the dark toward his thin sleeping mat. He could just make out the outline of Regulus' slumbering form on the left side of the tent.

"Have fun out shirking your duties?" Regulus muttered. Not asleep, then.

"Shirking? ...oh." Dresden cursed. "I had watch tonight. I forgot."

Regulus grunted.

"Did the captain notice?"

"Ha." Regulus snorted. "He's not a slob like Fletcher. He always notices."

They'd left Fletcher's troop after only three months. The group had quickly proved to be too dishonorable for Regulus' conscience. Not that anyone would have been eager to continue fighting side-by-side with the men who scarred their face. Dresden had stitched up the cut from the outside corner of Regulus' right eye down to his chin as best he could, but the scar was obvious. Regulus was ashamed of it despite Dresden's assurances it was masculine and intimidating. They'd been with Captain Samuelson's troop for nearly ten months, and even Regulus had made friends with the other mercenaries.

Dresden sighed. The captain was strict. There'd likely be some punishment for his missed shift. Hopefully not the lash. He winced at the thought. Samuelson was overall a good captain, but he had an over-strong belief in the effectiveness of the whip. But it was a first offense. Surely Dresden would only be put on manual labor, maybe struck with the rod. On the other hand, Samuelson had whipped a man last week for spilling a pot of stew. Granted, enough food for the entire troop had been lost to the cooking pit, but that had seemed harsh for an accident.

"I'll see the captain in the morning. Maybe if I go in bowing and scraping, he'll go easy."

"Don't bother." Regulus stayed comfortably reclined on his mat, but his words were short and clipped. "I talked to him. Just...keep your head down for a while. And pay better attention to your shifts, Jakobs."

Jakobs. Dresden recoiled. Regulus was ticked.

"And maybe invite me next time you run off to have fun," Regulus muttered.

"See, I would, but your stiffness around the ladies is off-putting." Dresden sat on his own thin mat and pulled his boots off in the dark. "Your refusal to get too close to a lady you see no chance of marrying ruins all the fun."

Regulus grunted. "Excuse me if I don't want to bring any more bastards or fatherless children into the world."

Dresden rolled his eyes, even as he felt a twinge of sympathy. He scratched at his beard. "Kissing a girl won't get her pregnant, you stick-in-the-mud."

"Just go to sleep."

He pulled off his belt, and his small coin pouch spilled as he tossed the belt aside. "Damn." He fumbled in the dark. "Where's the lantern?"

"Clean it up in the morning." Irritation rang in Regulus' low tone.

"Yeah, if I want to put a hole in my foot." Dresden found the lantern and the steel and flint next to it. "She gave me her brooch, and if I step on that pin in the morning, I won't be happy." He struck the flint, trying to light the lantern.

"Then feel for it," Regulus snapped. "I'm tired, and I don't want a light."

"Then turn your head," he snapped back, still working on the flint.

"Leave the light and go to sleep!" Regulus didn't move, but fury and something else tinged his rushed words. Something almost like apprehension. The wick finally caught, and the lantern slowly blazed to life.

"What is your..." Dresden trailed off as he looked over at Regulus.

Regulus lay on his stomach on his mat, shirtless and without his cloak that doubled as a blanket, his head turned away toward the tent wall. Dresden's abdomen clenched sharply as he took in the blood covering Regulus' back. Much of it had dried and clotted, but some of the stripes were still oozing.

"I told you to leave the light," Regulus mumbled.

Dresden dropped the flint, his stomach lurching and face burning. "Were you lashed?"

"Whatever gave it away."

"Why?"

Regulus was silent and didn't move. Finally, he sighed. "Find your precious brooch and go to sleep."

He'd tried to hide his lashing. Which was ridiculous. Even if he could have left the tent before Dresden woke in the morning, he couldn't hide it long. Which meant Regulus just didn't want to talk about it right now. Regulus was a model mercenary, and Captain Samuelson seemed to like him. What in creation could he have done that he was so ashamed to admit? It wasn't like Regulus would chide Dresden for forgetting guard duty if he'd done—

No.

"Don't bother. I talked to him."

"Regulus." His voice was choked and weak, and he had to clear his throat. "Tell me those weren't my lashes."

The only answer was the slow rise and fall of Regulus' back. The flicker of the lantern glittered in the blood. Dresden's breathing went shallow, his lungs seizing. *No.*

"Why would you do that, you idiot?"

"Go to sleep."

Dresden gulped. "I'll be back. I'm getting fresh water to clean your back. You still have that watered wine? I'll cut up some bandages once you're clean. I..." He rubbed his forehead. "Regulus, why?"

A pause. "I'm working on a full-body scar collection."

"That's not funny."

Regulus didn't respond, so Dresden pulled on his boots and left to get water, mentally cursing himself the whole way. He nearly ran into Ivan returning from his watch. Ivan blocked his path, which wasn't hard. The blond was built like a wall.

"Lieutenant Ivan." Dresden moved to go around Ivan, but Ivan shoved him back. "What's—"

"Where the hell were you?" Ivan's Segiledan accent, all choppy consonants and indistinct vowels, was extra clipped tonight.

Dresden's face heated. "I—"

"Have you seen Regulus?" Ivan shoved him again. "Have you?"

"Yes." He hung his head. "I'm—"

Ivan snorted. "Twenty lashes. Ten for the missed watch. Five for leaving camp without permission. Five for lying to the captain and saying he was the one who forgot his shift. He could have had just the five. He convinced the captain to give him yours, too. Said he could handle it better, and that it'd still convince you to mind your watches."

Dresden grimaced. *Regulus, you colossal idiot.* "I need water for his back."

"I like you," Ivan growled. "But Regulus might be the only truly honorable man I've ever met. Not to mention one of the best swordsmen I've ever seen. And he saved my life against that berserker tribe last month and saved all our hides when he figured out that Vaneltian ice serpent's weakness and killed it. So let me tell you." Ivan seized Dresden's shirt and pulled him in close. "None of the men are pleased with you right now."

"If it helps," Dresden said quietly, "I'm not pleased with myself."

Ivan grunted and shoved him back. "I've half a mind to beat you—except Regulus would probably pay me back in kind." He shook his head. "I don't know how you earned his loyalty, but I hope you're grateful for it."

Ivan strode past, letting his shoulder knock into Dresden.

Grateful, and ashamed.

Dresden hurried back to the tent with the water and dunked the only clean rag he had into the bucket. He eyed the caked layer of blood. "Did no one clean it?"

"I came straight here. I didn't want to look weak."

Dresden's mouth went dry. "Trust me, no one thinks you're weak." He began to rub at the blood and Regulus convulsed, then gripped the edges of his mat. Dresden continued to wipe away dried blood, wincing as some of the worse lines bled afresh. "They're all angry with me, though."

"Wha—" Regulus sucked in a sharp breath and jerked as Dresden washed away more crusted blood. His hands shook as they held the mat. "What?"

"I ran into Ivan. Sounds like everyone thinks I don't deserve a friend like you." A pang in his chest accompanied the admission. As he cleaned Regulus' back and thought about every time Regulus stood between him and Hendrick or Lord Kimberly, he thought he might agree. None of those had been this bad, though. He'd thought that belting so many years ago had been terrible. This was far worse.

Regulus didn't respond. Maybe he agreed, too. Dresden finished wiping off Regulus' back as best he could with new blood seeping out. He dug the watered wine out of Regulus' belongings.

"This is going to sting."

Regulus' hands tightened on the mattress and his entire body tensed. Dresden carefully poured a little wine over the cuts. Regulus groaned through clenched teeth, his muscles bulging as he braced against the pain. Every twitch, every anguished moan into the mat, stabbed at Dresden's heart.

He set aside the wine bag and grabbed his spare cloak. He had no bandages, so he'd make some. The sound of ripping fabric filled the tent.

"You're going to have to sit up so I can wrap these around you."

Regulus sighed. He pushed off the ground with a stifled whimper. "Thanks."

Dresden gripped the wide, long strips of dark fabric, staring at the raw lines crisscrossing Regulus' back. "Thanks? Damn it, Regulus, this is the least I can do. You shouldn't have—"

"You're my friend," Regulus said quietly. "Don't listen to the others. They don't understand."

"Understand what?"

"Why I can't watch you be hurt." Regulus shifted and grunted in pain. "You've stood by me when I was alone. They don't know... I have to..." He fell silent.

Dresden sighed and wrapped the strips around Regulus' torso and over his shoulders, tightly binding his back. Regulus kept wincing and clenching his hands, but he sat still despite the gasps and grunts.

"Done."

To his surprise, Regulus didn't lay back down. Instead, he turned around. "Any of the men give you grief, tell me?"

"I don't need you to protect me."

Regulus winced. "I know. That's not what I meant. I don't..." He pursed his lips, then shook his head. "Can you make sure I wake up on time for the dawn shift?"

"What?" Dresden gawked. "Captain didn't take you off watch?"

"He was going to. I said I could handle it."

"What exactly are you trying to prove?"

Regulus glanced away. "Habit, I guess."

Dresden frowned. Under Kimberly's guardianship, Regulus had trained harder and longer than anyone, pushed himself constantly, refused to show weakness. He'd finally admitted he thought if he could be strong enough, he'd prove his blood didn't make him inferior. They said his mother's peasant blood had diluted him. Made him less. Regulus insisted it made him stronger. He was always trying to prove he wasn't just as good as his cousins; he was better. Regulus had been trying to prove himself and admit no weakness for so long, he couldn't stop.

Dresden scratched the side of his head. "You don't need to prove anything. I'll take your shift in the morning. And any others until you're healed."

"You don't owe me—"

"Don't I? Your prideful self took a lashing for me and Etiros only knows why!"

Regulus slumped, then gasped and straightened again. "I couldn't watch you be hurt."

"And what, I'm a terrible friend who won't care that you're hurt?" Dresden massaged his forehead. He was being harsh for no good reason, but he couldn't comprehend why Regulus would do this. "Ivan said you told the captain you could handle it better. Do you think I'm too weak to survive a lashing?"

Regulus grimaced. "No, of course not. I just thought... I owed you."

"You...owe me?" Dresden blinked.

"Seven years," Regulus mumbled without looking at Dresden. "How many 'yes, master's does each lash erase? I don't know. Not enough. Maybe none. But old instinct, regardless. Protecting you. I don't have anyone else."

For a moment, Dresden didn't know how to respond. He stared at Regulus' downcast face, his tongue thick in his dry mouth and his chest tight. "Reg. I wouldn't have come with you if I resented you. I was your servant. That's just how it was. You could have treated me however you wanted, and you treated me like a friend."

"A friend doesn't go by master."

"A master doesn't take a beating for a servant, either," Dresden snapped. "Yes, I hated calling you that. I didn't like being the servant boy, I hated that my contract made me little more than a slave. But I hated the Kimberlys, never you. You released me from my contract when you could have forced me to come with you." Regulus glanced up and frowned, looking puzzled. Dresden shook his head with a dry chuckle. "But that didn't even occur to you, did it? That's why I'm still here. Because you're my friend, and I swear, one day, I'm going to take a beating for you and we can be even."

"I hope not." Regulus offered a wry smile. "If I earn my own beating, my reputation as a straight-laced stick-in-the-mud will be ruined." He adjusted a bandage. "But I meant it, Drez. I don't want to see you hurt."

"And I don't want to see you hurt. I hate it." *I hate myself for causing it.* He moved back to his own mat and cleaned up his spilled coins and the little brass circle brooch. Regulus slowly laid back down, poorly muffling his grunts and moans. With one last regret-filled glance at Regulus, Dresden snuffed out the lantern. "I suppose I just will have to be on my best behavior, so neither of us ends up lashed."

CHANGES

Age: 21
Location: Geirah

"Lieutenant Hargreaves, I want to talk to you." Captain Samuelson motioned for Regulus to stand with his left hand. His right arm was back in a sling across his torso, as it had been often since the troll attack a couple months ago. "In my tent."

Dresden stopped laughing at a joke one of the other men had told. Ivan stood as well, but Samuelson shook his head.

"Just Hargreaves, Lieutenant Cheznik."

Ivan's thick blond brows wrinkled, but he sat back down. The campfire quieted as Regulus followed the captain. Dresden gulped down the watery slop the cook dared to call stew. In four years, Regulus hadn't landed himself in trouble once—other than the time he took Dresden's lashing. Dresden had done a good job of not earning another since. Seeing Regulus' raw back was enough to convince Dresden he never wanted a lashing, and more importantly, he wouldn't risk Regulus sacrificing himself again because of some pig-headed notion he needed to earn Dresden's friendship.

Regulus had more than just not gotten in trouble, though. A year past, Samuelson had made Regulus his second lieutenant. But the fact Samuelson wanted to talk to Regulus alone, in his tent, without even Ivan, his first lieutenant... An unsettled feeling coiled in Dresden's gut.

"I thought Regulus and the captain were on good terms," Perceval mused. A muscular twenty-eight-year-old Monparthian man who'd recently joined with another Monparthian named Caleb, Perceval scowled more often than he smiled, but he got on well with Regulus. "What did he do?"

Everyone looked at Dresden. "Nothing, so far as I know."

That made him more nervous. Was there something Regulus hadn't told him? He finished his meal quietly, not even listening to the conversation around him as he kept glancing in the direction of the captain's tent. As he listened for the crack of the whip.

Someone rounded a tent, and Dresden sat up straighter. The captain walked over with Regulus. Regulus' face was impassive, but he looked fine. He walked at the captain's side, not following in subservience or being driven ahead.

"Gather round, men! I need everyone's attention!" The captain waited while word spread, and the mercenaries crowded in with low mutters.

Dresden tried to catch Regulus' gaze, to determine if everything was okay. But Regulus looked straight ahead, his arms folded over his chest. His sword still hung at his side. That was a good sign.

The captain held up a hand, and the men quieted. "Can everyone hear me?" he called. "This is important."

A low murmur of yeses passed through the crowd of twenty men. Regulus watched the captain, his expression still unreadable. What was going on?

"I'm afraid my arm has continued to worsen," Samuelson announced. "And I'm getting old. Accordingly, I'm retiring."

There was a startled murmur at this, but the captain held up his hand again.

"Regulus Hargreaves will be taking over as captain."

Dresden's mouth fell open.

"I'll stay for a couple weeks to help with the transition," the captain continued. "But Hargreaves is your captain, from this moment forward."

"Why don't we get a say?" a man shouted.

Ivan shoved the man over so quickly, Dresden wasn't sure who it was. "Idiot," Ivan scoffed.

"If you don't like it, you're free to leave," Regulus said with a shrug.

"Do you have a better idea?" the captain asked drily. "Someone else you would rather see take my place?" He looked around the men, his gaze challenging them.

A slight smile tugged at the scarred corner of Regulus' mouth. "If anyone does think they would be a better captain, they are free to challenge me for the right to lead. I will step down if anyone beats me in a fair fight."

Dresden barely managed not to laugh. Some of the men grumbled under their breath. Perceval stood, and everyone went silent. Dresden's mirth vanished. Perceval and Regulus had dueled only once—and ended the match in a tie when Samuelson called it off.

"Stop grumbling," Perceval said. "You all trust him, and you all know it makes sense." He nodded at Regulus. "Pardon the interruption, Captain Hargreaves." No one spoke as Perceval sat back down.

"That's what I thought," Captain—no, just Samuelson—said. He looked to Regulus. "Anything to add, Captain?"

"Plan's still to head out just after dawn tomorrow." Regulus nodded at the men. "As you were."

The men returned to their various campfires and conversations as Regulus and Samuelson said something to each other, then clasped hands. Samuelson headed back toward his tent. Ivan went to Regulus and clapped him on the shoulder, said something that made Regulus laugh, then returned to the fire. Regulus left for their tent, and Dresden followed.

"A minute of your time, Captain?"

Regulus paused halfway into their tent and grinned, his scar puckering near his mouth. "Come on in."

They ducked into the tent, and Regulus settled on his mat. Dresden sat next to him, then wondered if that was proper. Fear shot through his excitement for his friend. For four years, they had been equals. Would their friendship change?

"Bit unexpected," Regulus said. "Right?"

Dresden shrugged. "I didn't see it coming, but as much as the cap—I mean, Samuelson relies on you, I should have. Congratulations, Reg. Captain." He smiled, but suddenly *captain* tasted an awful lot like *master.*

"So, Drez, I have a question for you." Regulus clapped his hand on Dresden's shoulder. "I need lieutenants. I was thinking you first, and Ivan second. What do you say?"

"I..." Dresden gaped at Regulus. It wouldn't be equals. But it would be close. "Won't the men accuse you of favoritism?"

Regulus snorted. "Let them. You're one of the best fighters in the troop, Drez, and your insight is valuable. Ivan won't argue with me. You'll do great, and they'll respect you. And if not, they'll learn to."

Dresden frowned. "You've never been much for...discipline."

"I can be." Regulus dropped his hand from Dresden's shoulder. "And there are more ways to discipline than a whip."

"Are things...going to be different?"

"What do you mean?" Regulus frowned, looking genuinely confused. "I plan on running things about the same. Maybe a bit tighter, but with fewer lashings. Going to have more stringent rules about behavior and who I let in or let stay; and might be pickier about contracts. But otherwise, it'll just be that Samuelson is gone. Don't plan on kicking a bunch of men out or anything, if they're worried about that."

"No, I meant..." He shifted. "Us. Not quite equals, right?"

Regulus' brows lifted. "Oh. We won't need to act different. I mean, I guess I can't have you question me in front of the men, because that might undermine my authority, but you can always speak freely."

"Can I call you Reg?"

Regulus opened his mouth, then closed it. His shoulders slumped. "I hadn't thought about it." He shook his head. "No, it's fine. It's what I prefer. I mean, Captain would be good in an official capacity. In front of benefactors or in response to orders, but...it's not like someone is going to... There's no Kimberly here."

"Okay. Good." But Dresden's mind was stuck on *in*

65

response to orders. He'd gotten used to not being ordered around by his best friend. Even as a lieutenant, Regulus had rarely had to give him orders. He mostly just supported and advised Samuelson. But now Regulus' word would be law. It felt like backsliding.

"You'll always be my friend," Regulus said quietly. "I had you when I had no one."

"I know." Dresden bit his cheek. *Please don't forget it, Regulus.*

Please don't change.

CRIME & PUNISHMENT

Age: 21
Location: Hedengal

Dresden took a deep breath, his hand tapping against his leg. This was going to be bad. He'd put it off long enough. Another deep breath, and he lifted the flap to Regulus' tent. "Captain?"

Regulus sat on his low cot, reading a letter. He looked up and grinned. "Drez! Run into any trouble? Thought you'd be back a while ago."

Dresden gulped. "I'm sorry, Captain." He hung his head as Regulus' smile slipped. "I...take full responsibility."

"Re... For what?"

"We made a quick stop. At the tavern." His stomach churned as shame made his hands slick. Only six months since Regulus had become captain, six months of Dresden being lieutenant, and he'd messed up. Badly. And their new roles had been going so well. "I got distracted. The men followed my example. The supplies were not properly attended. We were...robbed." His throat stuck.

"How bad?" Regulus asked quietly.

"We brought back one sack of supplies. And...no coin."

For a moment, Regulus didn't speak. Then he cursed,

more than Dresden had heard him curse in nearly eleven years combined. He threw something, and Dresden closed his eyes, too ashamed to look Regulus in the eye. The tent went silent.

"Drez..." Regulus cursed again. "Do you know what I'm most upset about? Losing the supplies and coin is bad. It's going to cause problems, including discipline problems. But that's not the worst. You're right in taking responsibility."

I know. Dresden scuffed the toe of his boot into the ground. *Because taking full blame is what you would have done, even if it wasn't your fault.*

Regulus sighed, sounding unhappy. "I can't let this go, Drez. This kind of negligence..."

Dresden nodded. He'd known before he walked into the tent. "You'll need to make an example."

Regulus cursed. "I don't..." He groaned and kicked something, but Dresden kept his eyes locked on the ground. "I can't take this one for you! I'm the one that has to do it!"

"It's okay, Reg. I deserve it." He forced down the lump in his throat.

Regulus exhaled loudly and rubbed his hand over the side of his face. His face was flushed, his eyes anguished. He'd been a merciful captain. The whip had left his tent once in six months. But losing supplies through negligence was tantamount to stealing. And the punishment for stealing was clear. Regulus glanced toward a bag in the corner of his tent. A bag Dresden knew held the whip.

"No. No, I can't." Regulus shook his head fiercely.

"The men will talk." Dresden rubbed the back of his

neck. "You'll look weak. You can't afford that right now." He stared at the packed dirt. "Samuelson would have done it already if it were you, and you wouldn't have argued."

"I didn't take beatings for you in the past so I could beat you myself now." Regulus sank onto his cot and held his head in his hands. "If I wouldn't do it to you, I shouldn't do it to anyone. I'll replace whipping entirely. I've already been moving in that direction."

Dresden worked his throat, trying to get his voice to cooperate. "The men need to fear their captain."

"The men need to respect their captain." Regulus looked up. "I don't want you to fear me, Drez. I don't want you..." He turned away. "To hate me."

"I won't hate you. And will they respect their captain if he plays favorites?"

Dresden didn't know why he was advocating for his own lashing. Maybe it was old guilt over watching Regulus take his punishments. The lashing had been the worst. But Regulus had often stepped in front of Hendrick's fist or accepted a kick or slap when he claimed responsibility for something Dresden had done—spilled wine, a broken vase, unpolished armor. There had been other times as mercenaries when Regulus had taken a rod across the shoulders that should have been Dresden's.

"I know the punishment for what I've done, Captain." Dresden forced his feet to the corner and pulled out the whip. He flashed back eight years as he held it out to Regulus. *We are not equals. Again. A servant and his master. A captain and his soldier.* But this time, Regulus couldn't take his punishment. And Dresden wouldn't want him to. "I brought this on myself. And it's overdue, anyway."

Regulus took the whip, making Dresden's heart twist. "Outside, Jakobs. Tell the men to gather on the east side of camp."

Dresden nodded and slipped outside. The other men from the trip into town waited not far off, looking terrified. They eyed him sympathetically as he instructed them to gather the rest of the mercenaries. His feet felt heavy as he walked across camp, stopping to leave his scimitars in the tent he shared with Ivan. It had been folly to think they could be friends as they had before Regulus was captain. Just as it had been folly to think they could be true friends when Dresden was an indentured servant.

The rest of the mercenaries gathered in a group, keeping their distance from Dresden. He stared at a fir tree. Its lowest branches were a few feet above his head, and dead needles covered the ground at its base. The trunk was narrow, but probably wide enough he could brace himself against it. He rolled his shoulders, trying not to wonder what the whip would feel like.

"The men who accompanied Lieutenant Jakobs to town, step forward." Regulus' voice was hard, authoritative. His captain voice.

The men who had accompanied him shuffled forward. Dresden glanced at Regulus, then blinked. Regulus held a rope, but no whip.

"You all failed me and failed this company by allowing our supplies to be taken." Regulus' gaze roved over the men; his scarred lips curled down in displeasure. "Accordingly, you will have no supper. But as Lieutenant

Jakobs has assumed full responsibility, he will take the full punishment for the crime of depriving his company of supplies.

"Negligence that results in loss to this troop cannot be tolerated," Regulus continued. "Misuse of funds is theft, and careless stops at taverns while on duty is un-acceptable. And my lieutenant in particular should have done better. You all know the punishment for stealing."

Low murmurs.

"You also know I've never liked the whip. Which is why I will no longer use lashings as punishment."

Dresden jerked his head up. "Captain?"

Regulus turned his scowl on Dresden, but there was sorrow in his eyes. "You said you were distracted in the tavern. Tell me, Jakobs, was she worth it? She must have been very pretty."

The men snickered. Dresden's face heated.

"She was beautiful, Captain. And not worth it." *Not worth our friendship.*

"I've decided your punishment. Take off your clothes."

"What?" Dresden blinked, then lowered his head. "I mean, yes, Captain." He stripped down, his face burning as the rest of the men joked and laughed. Regulus silenced them with a look.

Regulus stepped forward, holding up the rope. "You'll spend the night here." He tied the rope to Dresden's wrist, then led him over to the fir tree without meeting Dresden's eyes. He tossed the rope over a low branch and tugged, pulling Dresden's right arm above his head. He grabbed Dresden's left wrist and tied it to the other end of the rope above his head. "No food, drink, or fire. He is to be left here, unbothered, but un-aided, until dawn."

Dresden let his chin fall to his chest. It was a mercy, in a way. The Hedengalese nights this time of year were chilly, but not unbearable. He would be cold and un-comfortable. He wouldn't sleep, and if he did, he'd likely be awakened by pulling on his wrists and shoulders. His shoulders would ache in the morning even if he managed to stay firmly on his feet all night. The effects wouldn't last as long or be as painful as a lashing. But the humiliation as he stood there stripped down to his thin, short braies was almost worse.

"Dismissed," Regulus barked. The men laughed and a few tossed out some insults as they turned back to camp. Regulus stood still and silent. Probably trying to figure out what to say.

"Thank you." Dresden curled his toes into the dead fir needles and cool dirt. "It's less than I deserve."

"It's more than a friend should do." Regulus rubbed the back of his neck. "But I'm your captain, too."

Never equals. A rueful laugh escaped before Dresden could stop it. A chill breeze stirred his hair, and he shiv-ered. It was going to be a long night.

"I gave orders to be careful of the coin and supplies." Regulus sounded irritated. "I trusted you with this. And as you said, you knew the punishment, you brought this on yourself. If you'd just followed orders, Jakobs..."

"Yes, master." Dresden's eyes widened as he realized what he'd said. He had spent so long as a youth and young man responding to Regulus saying "Jakobs" with a rote *yes, master.* Apparently that habit wasn't dead so much as buried. "I... I didn't..."

Regulus went rigid. For a moment, he hardly seemed to breathe, then his posture crumpled. He gulped. "I'm sorry, Drez. I'm truly sorry." He strode away, leaving Dresden with the rope around his wrists, the fir needles poking the soles of his feet, and the growing shadows as the sun slipped toward the horizon.

Light had scarcely begun to chase away the darkness and the sun had yet to breach the horizon when Regulus strode across the grass. Early morning fog swirled around his legs. Dresden watched his approach, shivering. His arms ached and shoulders pinched. His fingers were stiff with cold. Exhaustion weighed down his heavy eyelids, but every time he'd come close to falling asleep, pain in his shoulders or wrists had woken him.

Regulus held a dark bundle under one arm. His expression was unreadable. But as he drew closer, Dresden noted the hard line of Regulus' shoulders. The tension along his jaw and temples, indicating he was clenching his teeth. And the shadows under his eyes, suggesting he'd hardly slept. He set down the bundle on the dew-moistened grass and drew his dagger. Dresden shivered violently.

"I'm sorry, I'm hurrying," Regulus whispered. He cut free one wrist, and Dresden groaned as his arms fell to his side. His muscles prickled and his arm felt heavy. Regulus cut free his other wrist. Dresden's teeth chattered. "I'm sorry, one second."

"S-st-stop ap-apol-apologiz-izing." Dresden tried to rub his hands over his arms, but his muscles didn't want to cooperate.

"Here." Regulus snatched up the bundle and shook it open. He wrapped the thick wool blanket around Dresden and pulled it tight.

Dresden gripped the blanket, holding it as close as possible. Warmth enveloped him, easing his tight muscles despite the chill air nipping at his ears and face and creeping up under the blanket.

"Come on." Regulus gripped Dresden's shoulders and led him toward camp.

Dresden stumbled into a tent, and Regulus vanished, only to reappear a moment later and shove Dresden's clothes at him. The clothes were hot— Regulus must have placed them near the fire burning outside his tent. Dresden was tempted to just hold the bundle of warm fabric against his chest and curl up on his mat, but he forced himself to get dressed. Regulus watched, his mouth pressed into a thin line. Dresden moved to sit on his mat to pull on his boots, but instead saw Regulus' cot. He sunk onto the edge of the cot as a wave of exhaustion hit him. His arms were so tired.

"Drez?" Regulus ventured quietly.

He just nodded, staring at his boots next to his stockinged feet.

Regulus shifted. "Do...you want breakfast?" Dresden shook his head. Eating porridge sounded like more work than it was worth. Regulus nodded, uncertainty in his eyes. "Okay. Just...try to sleep, then. Your shift was moved to this evening."

"Wrong...tent—"

"No. Lie down. Sleep." Regulus' tone didn't allow an argument, even if Dresden had felt like giving one.

Dresden gratefully collapsed onto Regulus' cot and

curled up to preserve his body heat. Regulus sighed and stepped forward. Only when Regulus pulled the wool blanket over him did Dresden realize he'd forgotten about it on the ground. Regulus moved to leave.

"Reg…" Dresden's voice croaked, and he cleared his throat. "Reg." Regulus froze before the tent entrance. "I don't blame you."

Regulus' shoulders sagged, an expression like relief softening some of the hard lines of his face. Dresden wanted to say more, but he felt so warm and comfortable, his eyes drifted shut. He tried to talk, but his words slurred.

"You did the right thing. Thanks…blanket. Warm clothes. Cot. Didn't have to… Not necessary, Captain…" He let his weariness and the ache in his back and arms pull him toward sleep. After a moment, he heard Regulus whisper.

"Drez?"

He was too tired to respond.

Regulus was so quiet for so long, Dresden thought he must have missed him leaving. He was nearly asleep when Regulus whispered again.

"I know I don't deserve to call you my brother," Regulus murmured. "But that's what you've always been to me. I'll keep trying. I'm sorry for failing you again, brother." The tent flap rustled shut.

Brother? Dresden pulled the scratchy wool blanket in closer. *Of course you're my brother…*

HORSE THIEF

Age: 24
Location: Bhitran coast

Dresden stumbled sideways into a display of colorful, ornate carpets. The merchant waved him away, talking agitatedly in Bhitran, his teeth flashing starkly white next to his ebony skin.

"Apologies—"

The merchant cut him off with what sounded like an epithet and another emphatic wave of his hand. Dresden pushed away from the rolled-up carpets, careful not to upset the display, and adjusted his heavy pack. His legs felt gelatinous, and the hard dirt of the dusty street seemed to tilt. As if fighting down the crowded street, through the alternating glaring sunlight and shade from tasseled awnings and tall sandstone buildings, wasn't difficult enough without the strange feeling in his legs after two weeks at sea.

"Don't worry." Perceval clapped Dresden on the shoulder and he nearly sent Dresden off balance again. "You'll get your land-legs back soon enough."

"How are you fine?" Dresden grumbled as they pushed through the crowded Bhitran marketplace. They jostled past dark-skinned Bhitrans and Motus, brown-skinned Khastallanders, red-headed Hedengali, and other olive-skinned Carasians. Perceval's pale complexion stood out the way Dresden did in Craigailte or inland Monparth.

Perceval shrugged. "I lived near the coast of Monparth, and my father owned a ship."

Dresden shook his head at a wrinkled old woman hawking dates. "Your father *owned* his own *ship*?"

Perceval grinned over his shoulder. "My father is a very wealthy lord."

"He what?" Dresden stopped. Someone walked into his back and muttered in what sounded like Geiran.

"Lord Isaac Williamson the Third," Caleb said, appearing on Dresden's left, "is only disappointed in two things: that he still isn't a baron, and the disgrace that is his second son, our own miscreant, Perceval."

Perceval spun around, his eyes narrowed and crooked nose wrinkled. "Rathburn! If you're going to spill my life story, at least do it *right*. He's not disappointed in me, he's disgusted and horrified."

"No, because *your* father would take you back. Mine forgot I existed. 'Did I have four sons? Nope, just the three, stop the will there.' He—hang on." Caleb ran a hand through his shaggy blond hair and licked his lips. "I spy a *beauty*. Wish me luck." Caleb slipped behind a cart drawn by a braying donkey and made for a young woman, her mess of black curls tied back with a bright pink scarf.

"Good luck." Dresden smirked and continued through the marketplace, the sharp scent of dried peppers assaulting his nostrils.

They passed a bare-chested Bhitran man with thick braids down to his trousers, entertaining a crowd for tossed coins. Dresden slowed as he passed the crowd.

The Bhitran wove blue light into a castle, then more light into a dragon. Fire exploded from the light-dragon's mouth and razed the castle. Dresden rolled his eyes. He'd seen a few mages since leaving Monparth. Most of them worked for wealthy households as healers, warriors, or horticulturists. Maybe it was just because Monparth hadn't had any mages since before Dresden was born, but using a gift that powerful for cheap tricks seemed a disgusting waste.

He and Perceval found their cook, a Craigan man named Lawrence, and a few of the other mercenaries as they wound through the busy marketplace. The crowds lessened as they approached the edge of town, and without the shade of stall awnings, the heat increased. They found Regulus and most of the rest of their company setting up tents near a busy well, surrounded by camels, horses, and even a few saddled desert eagle gryphons. Several horses were staked among their groups' tents.

Regulus finished hammering down a tent stake and straightened. As Dresden approached, he wiped the back of his hand across his glistening forehead. Dresden nodded toward the horses.

"Got the horses, then?"

"Had to haggle to get a halfway decent price, but I *refuse* to ride those long-legged beasts." Regulus jerked a thumb toward some sleeping camels.

"Honestly," Dresden said with a chuckle, "I would pay to see you ride one."

The scarred corner of Regulus' mouth twitched. "How much?"

"Fine, I wouldn't pay, but I might dare you."

"Probably for the best, captains shouldn't take bribes." Regulus turned and lugged his belongings inside his tent.

As Etiros-forsaken hot as the Bhitran day was, the night was downright chilly. Dresden huddled beneath his cloak, tossing and turning as Ivan snored on the other side of the tent. He didn't resent Regulus for taking the captain's tent alone, and it made sense to have both lieutenants in one place should Regulus need to find them quickly. But Dresden liked to think Regulus wouldn't have made them share a tent if he'd had any idea how loudly Ivan snored.

Some other sound caught his attention. He strained to hear it over Ivan's snores. A light clinking. Whispers. A horse's snort. Dresden threw back his cloak, snatched up his scimitars, and burst out of the tent without putting on his boots. A sliver of moon and countless stars provided dim illumination, but he caught the outline of a horse moving between tents, followed by another. He frowned. Why wasn't he hearing the hoofbeats?

He stole across the now cool sand-covered ground, keeping close to the tents. Who was on guard? The whisper of muffled footsteps drew him on. Dresden darted around a tent and raised his scimitars.

A Bhitran with close-shaved hair drew up short, his eyes going wide as Dresden raised his blade to the man's throat. A rope trailed from the man's hand to the horse behind him, with two more of their expensive horses tied in a line behind the first.

"Funny, I don't recall the captain giving an order to move the horses." Dresden tilted his head to the side. "Actually, I don't recall having a Bhitran in the troop."

The man dropped the rope and raised his hands. He shifted sideways.

"Ah, no moving!" Dresden brought up his other scimitar and positioned the blades on either side of the Bhitran's neck. "Mercenaries don't take kindly to theft of their belongings."

"I will go. Leave horses. Not return." The man's accent was thick, but he spoke clearly. He sounded young. In fact, as Dresden's eyes adjusted further to the dim light, the clean-shaven Bhitran looked no older than twenty.

"You speak Monparthian."

"Yes. Please. I am sorry. You take the horses, and I leave."

The tent behind Dresden rustled. "Who is talk— what is going on here?" Regulus yawned and walked over next to Dresden, his bare feet rustling across the sandy ground.

"Attempted theft of the horses, Captain."

The Bhitran lowered his head, careful of Dresden's blades. "I am sorry, Captain. Please. I leave the horses and go, and not come back again."

A moment passed, and the Bhitran looked up. Regulus tapped a bare foot against the sand. "You speak Monparthian well. What else do you speak?"

The Bhitran shrugged. "I speak Bhitran, Motu Bhitran, Khast, a little Hedengali, a little Geiran, and Monparthian."

"You got past my guards." Regulus spoke quietly, his tone revealing nothing. "How?"

The man flashed a quick smile. "The night is my friend. It hides me. I know how to move silently."

One of the horses pawed the ground, hardly making a sound. Dresden looked closer. He chuckled. "He wrapped the horses' hooves. No wonder I didn't hear hoofbeats."

"You got three horses to let you wrap their hooves without being caught?" Regulus couldn't entirely hide the impressed tone from his voice.

The Bhitran nodded. "Horses trust me."

"I see. If I tell my lieutenant to lower his swords, will you promise not to run?"

"Will you promise not to kill me?"

Regulus laughed. "No, I'd like to talk, and men talk far better with their heads attached to their bodies." He motioned for Dresden to lower his swords, and reluctantly, Dresden did so.

"What are you thinking?" Dresden kept his gaze on the horse thief, ready to move should the man try to run.

"That we need a translator."

Dresden's brows pinched. "He's a thief."

"Half the men in our troop are some brand of criminal, Drez."

Dresden opened his mouth to protest, but he wasn't wrong. Lawrence had killed a man in a barroom brawl. Perceval and Caleb seemed to be running from something, Etiros only knew what. The way he and Regulus had left Kimberly, some might argue they were acting like fugitives, too. Not to mention how many people equated mercenary with criminal, anyway.

"What's your name?" Regulus asked.

"Why?" The Bhitran shuffled his feet and glanced to the side. Dresden lifted the tips of his scimitars, just enough to be vaguely menacing without being directly threatening.

"I'm Regulus Hargreaves. This is my lieutenant, Dresden Jakobs. I'd like to know who I'm talking to."

The Bhitran's mouth twisted to the side, then he shrugged. "Jerrick Faras."

"Why were you stealing my horses, Faras?"

The man gulped loudly. "It's my job."

Dresden barked a laugh. "Thief is not an occupation."

"I steal, I get paid. Job." Faras shrugged.

"Why not get an honest job?" Regulus folded his arms. The horses shifted behind Faras. Dresden eyed them, worried they might run off while they were talking to this lowlife.

"Ha." Faras shook his head. "Get honest job, says the mercenary. Tell me, if you decide to be something else now, who would hire you? You have particular skill, and people distrust you, yes? It is the same. Once you steal, only criminals will hire a criminal."

Dresden snorted. "Why steal in the first place?"

Faras' eyes gleamed in the faint moonlight. "My family was poor, with many children. My father had great debt. I stole little things to help, got bolder. My father boarded horses, they trust me. I stole horses. Then I got caught, and I ran. But hard to find work. I was desperate, so I work for...you would say criminal lord, I think. Steal horses. People know, but I have not been caught. No one will hire me."

Trapped. Dresden felt a twinge of sympathy for the young man. Maybe Regulus wasn't crazy. Often mercenaries were running from a life they no longer wanted— just like Regulus did.

"Any good with a sword?" Regulus asked.

Dresden's gaze snapped to Regulus, but he quickly returned his attention to Faras.

Faras licked his lips. "Not exactly. I fight with a double-sided axe. I have won a few...how you say? Illegal street fights. With fists and with axe."

"I see." Regulus looked to Dresden. Dresden sighed and nodded. Regulus was going to do it regardless of if Dresden thought it was a good idea, anyway. Regulus turned back to Faras. "How would you like a new job? Travel, see the world? Be my translator and interpreter, use your axe and stealth as one of my mercenaries?"

Faras stuttered in Bhitran. "I mean...you...I..." He spoke Bhitran again, then switched back. "I tried to steal your horses?"

"Yes, and I'm impressed you got as far as you did." Regulus crossed his arms. "I could use your talents. We have a strict code that you will have to agree to. Break it, and you'll be thrown out. But—"

"Yes!" Faras fell to his knees before Regulus, making both Dresden and Regulus take a step back. "I will serve you."

"Now, hold on, it's more a contractual—"

Faras held up his hands in supplication. "If you had given me to guards, punishment for stealing horses is death. I owe you my life, Captain Regulus Hargreaves."

Regulus hesitated. "Well...that's a bit much." He yawned, reminding Dresden just how tired he was. A shiver went through Dresden as the threat passed and the excitement wore off, and without something else to occupy his mind, the cold pressed in again. Especially on his bare feet.

"Will...you be leaving soon?" Faras asked hesitantly. "Orem—my employer—will be unhappy that I am leaving. Better if he does not know."

"We're leaving in the morning, escorting a Hedengali merchant who is nervous about the tales he's heard of giant scorpion-snakes and aggressive desert gryphons and other Bhitran monsters—not to mention bandits." Regulus offered Faras his hand and pulled the man to his feet. "I'm going to sleep. We'll talk in the morning." Regulus disappeared back into his tent.

Dresden shook his head. "Leaves me to take care of things, I see. Let's put those horses back. I'll be checking on the guard to make sure they watch them. You'll have to find your own place to sleep tonight."

Faras shifted from foot to foot. "He...really will take me? A horse thief?"

Dresden held both scimitars in his left hand so he could pick up the lead to the first horse. "Yes, well, Regulus believes people are more than their circumstances. He'll give you a chance to show through your actions you can be a better man. But you fail that chance...you likely won't get another."

"That seems fair." Faras scratched his closely shorn hair. "He is good man."

"That he is." Dresden smiled. "As the men like to say—that's why he's the captain." *And it's why Regulus will always be my best friend.*

I just hope he's right about Faras.

PICKING UP STRAYS

Age: 26
Location: Segiledus

"This is unacceptable!" Regulus' shout echoed through the Segiledan noble's hall. "You lied about the nature of the contract."

Ivan, standing to Regulus' left, quickly translated. Dresden stood still and alert to Regulus' right, his arms hanging loosely at his sides but ready to draw his scimitars from their scabbards across his back if necessary. He glanced at the cluster of chained Segiledan men in the corner of the large wood hall. Guards kept them pressed close together.

Lexan, their Segiledan benefactor, steepled his fingers, his eyes steely. He spoke in Segiledan, his tone dismissive.

"You have your payment. Go," Ivan translated.

"I agreed to bring in criminals," Regulus snarled. "These men are not criminals, and now I have the blood of those who resisted on my hands."

Ivan translated, and Lexan responded coldly. Ivan looked to Regulus helplessly. "He says refusing to serve in his army is a crime, so they are criminals."

"They are farmers!" Regulus thrust his hand toward the group. "You told me a dangerous band of criminals was hiding in your forest, terrorizing your people. They *are* your people!"

The men hadn't spoken since they'd caught them. Not even to answer Ivan's questions as Regulus and Ivan grew more concerned with how the small group didn't look like criminals. Some were old. A couple were young boys. They were clearly afraid. But when Regulus handed them over to Lexan, one of the captives had fallen to his knees and begged. And when Ivan had translated for Regulus, it had been with rage that made his Monparthian thick and broken.

The men hadn't been terrorizing the people. They had hidden from a draft and were sneaking out at night to plough their families' fields and visit their women and children. Lexan's defense was he had to answer an affront from a neighboring lord and needed men for his army.

"Temporary," he had said. As if short-term conflicts didn't take lives.

"They are my people," Ivan translated sullenly, "and I will deal with them as suits me. Leave, mercenary, before I change my mind about permitting you to leave."

Regulus chuckled darkly. "What will you do with them?"

Ivan translated, and Lexan looked over at the peasant men. He shrugged.

"Young men, fighters," Ivan translated. His face was red beneath his shock of blond hair. "Old men, care for wounded. Boys, labor."

Regulus worked his jaw. His sense of justice was liable to screw up another contract. "And they will not be punished for resisting?"

Lexan leaned back in his ornate chair with a dismissive look as he responded.

Ivan hesitated. He looked at Regulus, anger in the hard line of his mouth, but worry in his eyes. "They will be."

Regulus looked at Ivan. "Did he say how? His answer was longer than yours."

Ivan sighed. "Lashings, Captain."

Dresden's mouth twisted to the side. Well, that did it. They weren't getting out of here without drawing steel.

"Lexan," Regulus said in a low voice, "the boys and the old cannot be whipped."

Ivan winced as he translated. Lexan scowled and clutched the arms of his chair as he shouted a response.

"You tell me what to do in my own hall, mercenary?" Ivan supplied.

Regulus crossed his arms. "Release the old men and the boys. Or I will not leave until I have released them all." The rest of the mercenaries shifted behind them restlessly. Ready. Dresden's fingers twitched in anticipation, but they were under orders not to draw weapons unless the Segiledans did so first.

Ivan nodded, for a moment looking concerned, then eagerness sparked in his eyes as he translated.

Lexan stood with a shout, and the Segiledan guards drew their weapons. Dresden drew his scimitars and spun them as the rustle of weapons being drawn sounded behind them. Regulus said calmly, "Strike to wound."

Dresden ran at the closest Segiledan guard. The man blocked Dresden's right scimitar, but as often happened, was unprepared for the second blade, which Dresden buried in the man's thigh. The Segiledan dropped his sword with a scream and fell back, clutching his bleeding leg. Dresden turned and dodged the axe of another guard. A few blocked blows, then Dresden spun around the man and sliced open his calves.

Lexan shouted something, and the few Segiledans still standing dropped their weapons and raised their hands in surrender. On the low dais, Regulus stood between two bleeding Segiledan guards, the point of his sword at Lexan's throat.

Lexan muttered something. Regulus looked around, and Ivan stepped around a guard who was clutching his arm to his stomach. Ivan returned his mace to his belt. "He says he will tell everyone Regulus Hargreaves turns on his benefactors."

A grim smile tugged on Regulus' scar. "Oh, no, Lexan. You will tell everyone that Regulus Hargreaves bested you in your own hall. You will tell everyone that Regulus Hargreaves protects innocents and will not serve corrupt men. And you will tell everyone that Regulus Hargreaves has the honor not to slit your throat just because he has the opportunity."

Ivan translated. Lexan clenched his jaw. The fury in his eyes said he would do no such thing. But the guards standing around with wide eyes? The chained men in the corner? The servants cowering along the walls and the handful of courtiers waiting in the back of the hall for their turn to speak to their liege? Oh, they would tell. And the type of men Regulus did not want to work for would likely avoid him. But benefactors looking for a mercenary troop with honor? They would be impressed, and they would hire Regulus.

It was a game Regulus had played before. It was why men who had never hired mercenaries hired Regulus. The troop's reputation for accomplishing contracts with deadly skill, and even more, Regulus' own reputation as a fearsome swordsman, got benefactors' attention. Regulus' honor earned their trust—or their distrust, in some instances.

A Carasian warlord had once hired them and been pleased to say he could do so while his rival desperately searched for another troop. "My enemy had the opportunity first," the warlord had said. "But he could not hire the righteous mercenary for fear you would smell out his corruption and destroy him." The warlord had grinned. "You will destroy him anyway."

And they had. The man had been ruthless and made his wealth off the slave trade. It was an instance were Regulus expressly told his men not to hold back.

Regulus' voice cut through Dresden's thoughts. "Someone get them out of those chains." Regulus sheathed his sword, his focus on Lexan. "This lord you have a quarrel with. Why, and what were your intentions?"

Dresden set about helping with freeing the prisoners while Regulus and Lexan talked with Ivan translating. Dresden removed the shackles from a thin boy of some thirteen or so years with knotted straw-colored hair above a sun-tanned face.

"Thank you, sir," the boy whispered as he rubbed his wrists.

Dresden's head jerked. "You're not Segiledan."

The boy shook his head. "I'm Monparthian. I came with my parents over the pass to sell wool."

"Where are your parents?"

The boy stared at his feet. "Dead. Troll. I hid."

"And the Segiledans took you in?"

The boy nodded, but he shuddered and glanced at a farmer standing near him. Dresden looked to the tall Segiledan. The man watched the Monparthian boy, lips pursed beneath his reddish-brown beard. He said something in Segiledan. The boy whimpered and nodded.

"You speak Segiledan?" Dresden asked the boy.

"Only a little." He glanced at the glaring farmer. "I've learned enough for orders."

"Orders?" Dresden crouched down to be at eye level with the boy and put a hand on his bony shoulder. "What—"

The farmer snapped something in Segiledan and grabbed the boy's shoulder, pulling him back and stepping between him and Dresden. Dresden straightened with a frown. The Segiledan said something else, his tone angry.

"What's he saying, boy?"

But the boy just shook his head.

"What's going on here?" Regulus strode over next to Dresden. "Why's this one look angry?"

"Don't know." Not that he didn't have his suspicions. He pointed around the Segiledan at the boy. "I was trying to talk to that Monparthian boy, and this one seems displeased."

"Monparthian?" Regulus' eyebrows rose. "Come here, lad."

The boy looked up at the Segiledan's back and shook

his head. The Segiledan said something, his tone challenging.

"He says the boy belongs to him," Ivan said, coming up on Dresden's other side. "The boy stole from him, so he works to pay off his debt."

Regulus frowned, then stepped to the side to see the boy. "What's your name?"

The boy hesitated. He looked at Regulus, at the farmer, then stared at the ground. "Harold."

"How'd you come to steal, Harold?"

"Orphaned."

Regulus' jaw tightened. "Do you like working for this man?"

Harold winced. "Yes." It couldn't have been a more obvious lie.

The Segiledan put a hand on Harold and said something. Dresden looked to Ivan.

"He thanks you for freeing them, but if Lexan allows them to return home, he will need the boy's help with the harvest."

"They're going home." Regulus nodded. "We will be retrieving the money Lexan's rival owes."

Dresden frowned. "You took another contract from Lexan?"

Regulus smiled wryly. "I convinced him it was better to pay us to fight his battle than try to get these hapless souls to do it. Wasn't hard after he saw us in action."

And that's why Regulus is the captain.

"Ivan, tell them they're all going home. No more draft."

Ivan translated Regulus' news, and the men looked stunned, then overjoyed. Regulus looked back at the boy.

"Do you want to go back to the farm with this man?"

Harold glanced nervously at the farmer, then nodded. "It's the closest I have to a home. It's pretty. By the mouth of the Ureld River."

Regulus pursed his lips. "Near the Darbot Forest?" Harold nodded. "Very well." He looked at the Segiledan. "Treat him well. And give him more food." Regulus turned as Ivan translated. "Move out men! We have another mission."

⌘

Raiding the other Segiledan lord's treasury proved easy. His men were unprepared for an attack, especially from a mercenary troop of fifteen. Regulus took half the Segiledan's treasury for Lexan. "Lexan won't know we didn't take it all," he said.

Lexan was borderline mousy when they returned. He clearly wanted them to take their payment and leave without any further trouble. Regulus was happy to oblige.

"Where to next?" Dresden asked.

"I fancy visiting Monparth," Regulus said. "Been nearly two years since our last contract there. I miss it sometimes. Is that ridiculous or what?"

"I'd like to see home again."

"Home?" Regulus looked at him in surprise.

"It's where we grew up. Doesn't that make it home?" Dresden frowned. "But I mean Monparth. Not the Kimberly estate. Never care to set foot there again."

Regulus laughed. "Agreed. Monparth it is. But first, we're going to swing slightly out of our way. There's something I want to check on."

⌘

The moss-covered small stone farmhouse standing in

94

the middle of the field of bright green grass looked picturesque. A clear blue sky stretched above the field of still-green grain behind the farmhouse. The fir trees of the Darbot Forest rose up beyond the fields, a shadowy backdrop to the pastoral scene.

Regulus and Dresden rode next to the Ureld River, the creak of their saddles drowned out by the gurgle of water over river stones. They'd left the men at the camp closer to the pass, and the day of riding alone had been peaceful. Times like this, Regulus felt like Dresden's friend more than his captain, and Dresden treasured those moments.

A shout split the calm air, followed by a cry. Regulus kicked his massive black warhorse to a gallop, and Dresden followed, racing toward the sound. They rounded the farmhouse as another cry echoed.

The tall Segiledan farmer stood over a small hunched form next to a basket of spilled eggs. The Segiledan shouted something and raised the thick stick in his hand. Regulus leapt off his horse with a roar. The farmer looked up, his eyes wide and brow pinched, as his makeshift club slammed into the boy's back. Regulus lunged into the man, shoving him to the ground. Dresden jumped down and went to the quaking body curled on the ground.

"Harold?" Dresden laid his hand gently on the dirty straw-colored hair. The boy twitched, then raised his head tentatively. Regulus knelt on Harold's other side.

"You..." The boy rubbed away his tears. "Why are you here?"

"I came to ensure you weren't being mistreated," Regulus ground out. "How long has he been hitting you?"

Harold whimpered and ducked his head. Dresden's hands curled into fists. The Segiledan farmer had risen to his feet, and he said something that sounded furious. Dresden stood, drawing one of his scimitars.

"I'd stay back if I were you." The man might not have understood his words, but he eyed the sword, clearly understanding that.

"Harold," Regulus said. "I'm in need of a baggage boy. How would you like a job?"

"A...job?"

"You won't make as much as the mercenaries, since you won't be doing the fighting," Regulus said. "But you'd be paid. Plenty of food." His face darkened. "No beatings."

Harold nodded rapidly. "Yes. Yes, please, sir, yes." He pushed off the ground and cried out, gripping his side.

Regulus' eyes flashed. He lifted the boy's tunic, revealing a large black-and-blue bruise. He touched the bruise and Harold jerked with a cry of pain, but Regulus continued to prod the bruise. "Just bruised. Feels like your ribs are intact." Regulus shifted and picked Harold up, holding the boys' thin frame to his chest as he carried him to his horse.

Back at the camp, Regulus went to plan their route through the mountains, leaving Dresden to take care of Harold. Dresden brought extra food, and Harold consumed it all like he'd been starved. Considering how bony the boy was, it seemed possible. After Harold had eaten, Dresden made him remove his tunic and slathered the bruises in numbing salve. The boy's ribs and spine jutted out from under his skin, and old and new bruises dotted his upper body.

"Dresden," Harold said uncertainly.

"Yes?"

"Why did..." Harold frowned. "What's his name? Reginald? The scary big man with the scar. He said it at the hall, but I can't remember."

Dresden laughed. "The scary..." He fell into another fit of laughter. "Reginald!" He tried to hold back his laughter when he saw the embarrassed blush on Harold's cheeks, but he couldn't help it. "Regulus Hargreaves. But you'll call him Captain."

"Oh." Harold pulled his tunic back on and winced. "Why did Captain help me?"

Dresden sobered, even though he wanted to laugh again at Harold saying Captain like that was Regulus' name. "The captain has a big heart, and he doesn't like cruelty."

"But..." Harold looked away uncomfortably. "Aren't you all mercenaries? Don't you...you know...kill people?"

"Yes." Dresden laid back on the ground. He'd given Harold his mat. He'd have to get a new one. "But we try to only kill bad people."

Harold nodded slowly. "That's why the captain was angry at Lexan. He thought the farmers were bad people, and they weren't?" He grimaced. "Most of them."

"Yes."

Harold looked deep in thought. "I think I like the captain."

Dresden chuckled. "Well, good. Disliking the captain is the fastest way to make sure you have no friends in this troop."

THE LETTER

Age: 26
One month later and one week after Regulus swears to
serve the Prince of Shadow and Ash (as revealed in the
novel Prince of Shadow and Ash*)*
Location: Thaera Duchy, Etchy Barony, Monparth

"Reg. Reg, talk to me. What's it say?"

Regulus didn't move. He stood in the exact same position he'd been in for the last few minutes, his back rigidly straight, his wide eyes glued to the letter in his hands. Dresden eyed the seal. A gryphon. He'd never paid much attention to the seals of the various noble families of Monparth, and he hadn't had cause to think on them in years, other than a few trips into Monparth for mercenary contracts. Like the one they had recently finished.

"Etiros above, Regulus, if it's not about a contract, what is it?"

"I...my..." Regulus blinked. The parchment trembled in his hands. "I'm..." He shook his head and his eyes scanned the letter yet again. "My brother is dead."

"Your...wait, your half-brother? The one you've never met?"

Regulus nodded. "It's from Baron Carrick. My father wrote me into his will."

"Your father...what?"

"He died a few years ago, apparently. My father."
Regulus' hands tightened on the letter. "According to
my father's will, if his legitimate son died without an
heir, the Arrano title and estate is to fall to...me. And
my half-brother is dead. Some horse-riding accident."
He finally looked up from the letter, his brow pinched
over shocked eyes. "I'm...Lord of Arrano."

Dresden gaped, his mouth stuck hanging open.

"They've been trying to track me down for nearly a
month." Regulus shook his head. "Baron Carrick is currently in Lerilton on business for the next week. I can
report to him there to pledge my fealty and accept
my...my title." Regulus swayed. He ran his fingers
through his hair, then rubbed the pommel of his sword.

"You're a lord." Dresden stared at Regulus. "Lord of
Arrano."

Regulus laughed, but it was bitter, angry. "I always
wanted to be welcomed at Arrano. But this...I never
dreamed of this." His eyes flashed and the parchment
crinkled as his hand fisted. "If this had come three
weeks ago..." He growled in irritation. "I wouldn't have
taken that job. I'd be free."

Dresden's gaze darted to Regulus' right arm, but the
mark the sorcerer had placed there was hidden beneath
his sleeve. "Well..." he said slowly. "You'll be a lord regardless. And once your debt is repaid, you'll just be a
lord."

Regulus snorted. "Assuming sorcerers keep their
word."

"He sounded sincere. And he's kept his word so far."

Regulus refolded the wrinkled letter. "Gather the
others." His face momentarily twisted with sorrow.

There were so few of them left.

Once the remaining four mercenaries plus Harold were gathered, Regulus stood before them with his hands clasped behind his back. "Men, I thank you for standing with me these last couple weeks." He worked his jaw. "I know I've only just returned, but...I will be leaving again."

Perceval swore. "He's sending you away again already?"

"No." Regulus smiled tightly. "This is a personal affair. I need to go into Lerilton." He licked his lips. "I will no longer be your captain."

"What?" several men cried at once.

"Captain—" Perceval started.

"I do not understand," Jerrick said, his arms crossed.

"Because of that Prince of Ash?" Estevan demanded.

Shadow and Ash, Dresden thought, but he didn't say anything.

"No." Regulus shifted. "I received a letter. Assuming this is not a trap, and I can convince Baron Carrick of my identity, I will no longer be a mercenary. I will be Lord of Arrano."

The men stared at Regulus, dead silent and clearly puzzled.

Regulus cleared his throat. "I have never talked about my past. My father was lord of a modest estate here in Monparth. Not far from here, actually. My mother was..." He tugged on the collar of his shirt. "A servant." He hurried on.

"My father and half-brother are dead, and I'm the only remaining heir. There is a chance Baron Carrick will seize the opportunity to take Arrano for himself by denying me. Which is why I will be going alone. If Carrick tries to kill me..." He swallowed. "I will be exposed and will have to go into hiding. If all goes well, I'll return. And at that time, I'll ask again if you wish to remain under my command."

Dresden started. He hadn't considered... If Regulus was a lord, where did that leave him? A guard? A freeman? A...servant?

"I know some of you have reasons for leaving life among the nobility behind." Regulus' gaze flicked over to Caleb and Perceval. "Some of you are used to lives of travel." He looked to Estevan and Jerrick. "So I will not blame you if settling down at Arrano is not for you." Regulus' left hand strayed to his right arm. "Or if you have second thoughts about staying under my command, given my...condition. Dismissed."

The mercenaries hesitated, then dispersed, except for Harold. Harold stepped forward uncertainly, his youthful face twitching with nervousness. "Captain?"

"Yes, Harold?" Regulus' expression softened.

Harold glanced at Dresden. Dresden wasn't sure what the boy wanted to say, but he nodded encouragingly. Harold looked back to Regulus. "Will there be a place for a baggage boy at Arrano?"

"No, I don't think so."

Dresden stared at Regulus, shocked. The boy had nowhere to go. Harold's shoulders fell. Dresden opened his mouth to ask Regulus what his problem was, but Regulus smiled.

"But if I'm going to be a lord, I will need a squire."

Harold choked. "A...squire?"

Regulus walked over and clapped the boy's bony

shoulder. "Think about it. If I come back, you can give me your answer. Now go on."

"Thank you, Captain." Harold darted into the camp.

Dresden tried to ignore the discomfort in the pit of his stomach. "And what about me?"

"What about you?"

He hesitated. Their relationship was shifting yet again, and he didn't know what to do about it or how to treat Regulus now. "I suppose you'll be...needing servants."

Regulus looked horrified. "Etiros, no, Drez." He glanced toward the tents and lowered his voice. "I didn't want to say anything, not before they've had a chance to think about it. To take the chance to leave. If they're not here when I get back...I won't blame them. If I get back."

"Say anything about what?" Dresden eyed Regulus suspiciously, trying to figure out what his friend was thinking.

"If I'm a lord...I can knight you, Drez."

Dresden gasped. "Reg, I—"

"Wait." Regulus held up a hand. "I'd want you to think about it. You'd be a knight. You'd have more rights. I'm not sure what the situation is at Arrano, but I could hopefully give you some land. But..." He turned away slightly. "I'd be your liege. You would owe me fealty. You would be tied to Arrano, and to me. I don't want you to feel trapped or...to come to resent me."

Dresden laughed. "You left me tied to a tree naked a few years back. If I was going to resent you, I think I already would. I can't resent you for ennobling me."

"You wouldn't really be noble. Not in the eyes of the

lords." Regulus looked to Dresden. "You would be to me. The others, too, if they accepted."

"You...would knight them all?" *Of course he would.* Because that's who Regulus was.

Regulus nodded. "If they agree. I'll need knights. Loyal men who know my secret. And friends. I'm going to need friends if this works out." He swallowed. "The bastard mercenary is unlikely to win many friends among the nobility."

"I don't need to think about it. I would have gone with you if you'd offered me a place as a gardener." Dresden smiled at the affronted look on Regulus' face. "You're my oldest friend, Reg. And the fact it wouldn't even cross your mind to offer me anything less than a knighthood, and that you would be concerned about making me subservient..." He shook his head. "You're a good man. Besides, you know how many times you've saved my life?"

Regulus chuckled. "Twelve. Well, nine. Three of those weren't mortal danger."

"Twelve?" Dresden blinked. "Hold up, that—"

"First, the time you fell in the river."

"The...I had that under control." Dresden's face heated. He hadn't. Not even a little. "You've been counting since we were children?"

"Not right away. I started counting after I took your belting." Regulus reddened. "I don't mean it like that. I..." He gulped and looked away. "I hoped you remembered...when I had to scold you in front of Lord Kimberly, or when you were wounded because you became a mercenary with me, or when I had to...discipline you as your captain. I counted the times I'd saved you, protected you. And I hoped that it somehow made up for the rest."

Dresden stared at Regulus. Ice settled into his stomach. "You've been afraid I'd resent you. Stop being your friend." Awareness weighed heavily on him. "You are my friend, Reg! You have been since that day you pulled me out of the river, and I realized you weren't like the other nobles. You cared. And even when I've been mad at you, even when I've resented that we aren't equals, I've never hated you. You're more than my friend. After everything we've been through, everything we've done for each other—don't forget, I've saved your neck on the field a few times, too—you're my brother, Regulus."

Regulus jerked. His gaze locked on Dresden, frozen. His throat worked and his jaw tightened. He blinked, opened his mouth, then slammed his quivering jaw closed. The emotion in Regulus' eyes twisted Dresden's heart, threatening to make him an emotional wreck, too.

"Brothers," Regulus whispered. "I'd make you a lord if I could do it, Drez."

Dresden smiled. "I don't need it. I'd be abominable at it, anyway."

Regulus chuckled, shaky and unsteady as a tear escaped from his eye. "I doubt I'll be any good at it."

"Anyway." Dresden clapped his hands, feeling uncomfortable with the raw honesty. "I'm coming with you to Lerilton. Things go well, I want to be there. Things go poorly, you're not going into hiding without me."

Regulus paled. "No. If things go poorly, you could be killed."

"I'm still going. My brother could need me."

"Dresden, please. I...I need to know you're alright. If I'm found out, I need to know you're safe, and I need to know you'll take care of Harold."

"Harold and Jerrick get on well, and none of those men would abandon Harold. I'm coming."

Regulus frowned. "I could order you to remain behind."

That hurt, but Dresden shrugged nonchalantly. "I could disobey."

"Oh, perfect, then my first act as a lord can be to tie you to a tree." But his words held no force, and Regulus' hand tapped nervously against his leg.

Dresden lifted a brow. "I'll take my chances that you'll forgive me."

Regulus cursed. "Fine. I'll be glad for the company, but if you get killed..." His hand fisted. "Just...don't get killed."

"I'll keep that in mind," Dresden replied dryly. But he saw the haunted look in Regulus' eyes. If Dresden was killed, Regulus would never forgive himself. *Best not die.*

MY LORD

A couple days later

Dresden followed Regulus and a guardsman into a private room at the tavern. The air smelled of ale and bodies kept too close together and straw mattresses that had suffered in the unusually humid summer. Dust mites floated in the air. The guard stepped to the side, his hand on his sword. Another guard stood in the room, and he straightened as they entered. His gaze swept over Regulus and Dresden, taking in their weapons, and his hand went to his sword as well. It was mildly amusing. Dresden cast an appraising glance at the guards. Either he or Regulus could take them both, easily.

"My lord Baron Carrick," their escort said, "this man claims to have business with you. Says his name is—"

"Regulus Hargreaves." Carrick stood from behind a tiny wood table covered in nicks, setting aside a piece of parchment and a quill. He nodded, his lips pursed as he examined Regulus. "I admit, I had rather hoped you either wouldn't show or would be an imposter. But you look more like Kenneth than his own son did."

To his credit, Regulus didn't so much as flinch or show a flicker of emotion at Carrick referring to his half-brother as his father's own son. As if Regulus wasn't really his father's son. Regulus gave a small bow.

"Baron Carrick." Regulus reached into the pouch at his belt and withdrew something metallic. "I wouldn't presume to attempt to claim my inheritance based on a passing similarity to Lord Kenneth Arrano." He held out his hand. The signet ring sat on his hand. "I would wager my father's will specified I would have that?"

Carrick's brows rose in surprise as he picked up and inspected the ring. "Yes...it did. Although, I didn't really expect you to have it after all these years."

Dresden tried not to gape. He didn't know Regulus still had that ring.

"Well then," Carrick handed the ring back. "You'll just need to swear your fealty, and I'll authorize the will, and legally, everything will be yours." Carrick stepped back. "Take a knee, Hargreaves."

Regulus' hand twitched, but he lowered to one knee and inclined his head. Dresden tensed, prepared to draw his scimitars if needed. But Carrick walked Regulus through the oaths of fealty to himself and to the king of Monparth, and no one made any threatening movements.

"Rise, Lord Hargreaves of Arrano."

Dresden held his breath as Regulus stood and bowed.

"Thank you, Baron Carrick."

Carrick nodded, then returned to the table. He sorted through some papers, pulled one out, and signed it. He handed it to Regulus. "You'll find the Ladies Arrano still living at the castle."

"Ladies?" Regulus asked.

"Your father's wife and your brother's wife." For the briefest moment, a dark smile flickered over Carrick's face. "I wouldn't be surprised if they challenge you."

"Challenge me?"

"In the case of your death, the estate would go to the elder Lady Arrano. As a woman, she cannot stake a claim while you live." Carrick shrugged. "But if she can find a man to challenge you on her behalf, she is permitted to do so."

"Oh." Regulus shuffled uncomfortably. "Thank you for the warning." He bowed again, and they left the small tavern room.

Once outside town, Regulus visibly relaxed. "That went better than expected."

"Congratulations, my lord." Dresden smiled, but Regulus tensed.

"Please, don't do that." Regulus' face contorted in distaste. "My lord reminds me of Lord Kimberly, or all these lords we've worked for who grow fat while they pay us to do what they're too lazy to do themselves. Or the sorcerer. And feels too much like master. Just Regulus or Reg. Please."

A warm feeling spread in Dresden's chest. "Sure, Reg."

Regulus frowned. "Might have Harold call me my lord, though. Last thing I need is for my squire to slip up and call some other noble 'sir' or something." He shrugged. "I'll let him choose."

The men were watching for their return and had gathered around before they had even dismounted.

"So?" Jerrick prodded. "Things didn't go completely wrong, since you're here."

"Am I looking at a mercenary or a noble?" Caleb asked.

Regulus held up the will. "According to this, a noble."

The men whooped and cheered. Regulus held up his hand to quiet them. "You're all still here." His voice was tight was emotion. "Will you...come with me? Serve me as Lord Hargreaves of Arrano?"

Perceval spoke first. "No one else I'd rather serve, Captain. Besides, Leonora will be thrilled. She's been trying to convince me to give up the life. Months to years gone at a time with no guarantee I'll return, or that she'll know if I won't, doesn't suit her. Or me, for that matter. She'll move to Monparth if it means I'm staying with her."

Jerrick grunted. "Honestly, I'd rather settle down. Maybe I'll meet a nice girl. If you'll have me, Cap—my lord."

"I've rather missed living in a castle," Caleb mused. "Besides which, you can't get rid of me that easily."

Estevan shrugged. "What else would I do? And I'd be dead a few times over if not for you. Or at least in prison somewhere." The men all chuckled at that.

"You already knew my answer, my lord," Harold said. He lifted his chin, determination in his eyes. Dresden noted his *my lord* with amusement. He was eager to prove he could be a good squire, and Dresden guessed Regulus would have difficulty getting Harold *not* to call him my lord.

Regulus looked over the small band, his eyes glistening. "I may be a lord, but I'm not my own man." His hand strayed to his right arm, rubbing at the mark under his sleeve. "You would continue to serve a slave?"

A chorus of yeses and protests that Regulus wasn't a slave answered. Regulus' shoulders sagged as he swallowed back his emotion. Dresden smiled. Regulus never believed he was good or worthy. Maybe he would see it now.

"I don't deserve friends like you." Regulus cleared his throat. "Dresden Jakobs." He turned toward Dresden and drew his sword. The men made sounds of confusion. "Kneel."

"What?" Estevan gasped.

Dresden smiled reassuringly at the men and dropped to one knee.

"I, Regulus Hargreaves, Lord of Arrano"—Regulus touched the flat of the blade to Dresden's shoulder—"by the authority invested in me as a lord of Monparth, hereby bestow upon you the title and bond of knighthood." He moved the sword to the other shoulder, looking hesitant. "Do you swear to uphold the laws of Monparth, the code of chivalry, and to...serve me faithfully as your liege?"

Dresden smiled, trying to let Regulus know it was okay. "I swear it."

Regulus lifted the sword as relief flickered in his eyes. "Arise, Sir Dresden Jakobs."

Sir Dresden Jakobs. Dresden's throat tightened with joy. He might never get used being Sir Jakobs. He bowed. "Thank you, Regulus."

The men applauded and a couple started to congratulate Dresden, but Regulus held up his hand. "Step forward and kneel, Perceval."

Perceval's face went slack. "Captain?"

"Not Captain, Perce. Regulus." Regulus motioned him forward. "Unless you want to serve me without a title, step forward."

Perceval quickly stepped forward and dropped to his knee. Regulus knighted him, then looked to Caleb. "Caleb, step forward and kneel."

"I...thank you, my lord."

Regulus smiled. "Regulus. Please. I want my knights...I want my friends to call me Regulus."

As soon as Caleb had been knighted, Regulus looked to Jerrick. "Step forward and kneel, Jerrick."

Jerrick's eyes widened. "Captain... My lord... Regulus?"

"Come on, man."

"But..." Jerrick shuffled his weight from foot to foot and looked down. "I'm Bhitran."

"And if you'd get on your knee, you'd be a knight of Monparth, too." Regulus lowered his sword. "I have no hesitation about knighting you, my friend. But if you would rather not—"

Jerrick quickly moved to kneel before Regulus. He looked up with tears in his eyes. "I would not have thought...I would have no other lord as liege."

Finally, Regulus turned to Estevan. Estevan looked uncertain. Nervous. "Step forward—"

Relief spread over Estevan's face and he practically lunged to kneel in front of Regulus. "Thank you. I won't let you down, Regulus."

"Did you think I would leave you out?" Regulus asked, his brow knit and gaze puzzled.

"I'm young and...a nomad with a criminal past." Estevan flushed. "I hoped...but I wouldn't presume."

Once Estevan was knighted, Regulus sheathed his sword and looked around at his men. Dresden's chest swelled with pride. What a long way Regulus had come from the boy who had wept against a tree trunk while his own cousin beat him. An accomplished and feared mercenary captain. A lord with loyal knights.

Perceval chuckled. "If ever I were to reenter the nobility, I couldn't have hoped for more deliciously scandalous fellow knights. This is going to be fun."

For a moment, Dresden worried Regulus would be offended or concerned, but Regulus laughed.

"The bastard and his group of misfit knights." Regulus looked over his men with a grim smile. "This should be interesting."

www.ingramcontent.com/pod-product-compliance
Lightning Source LLC
Chambersburg PA
CBHW020416130626
46549CB00006B/2585